PRAISE FOR *MAKING HEARTS*

"Wow! I've never read a book like this! Totally engrossing, *Making Hearts* is an absolute tour de force. Jack Getze has done himself proud with this work. I've never read a story with an infant as the protagonist and more—an infant who acts proactively against formidable opponents with overpowering advantages and wins out. This is a book of supreme imagination, originality and most of all—*heart*. I am in complete awe of Getze's talent displayed supremely in this work. This is the book the cliché— *you gotta read this!*—was invented for."

—Les Edgerton, author of *The Genuine,*
Imitation, Plastic Kidnapping; Bomb;
The Bitch and many others

MAKING HEARTS

BOOKS BY JACK GETZE

The Austin Carr Series
Big Numbers
Big Money
Big Mojo
Big Shoes

The Black Kachina
Making Hearts

JACK GETZE

MAKING HEARTS

Down & Out Books
3959 Van Dyke Road, Suite 265
Lutz, FL 33558
DownAndOutBooks.com

The characters and events in this book are fictitious. Any similarity to real persons, living or dead, is coincidental and not intended by the author.

Cover design by Bob Babcock

ISBN: 1-64396-156-X
ISBN-13: 978-1-64396-156-9

ONE

Everyone at the dinner party laughed and teased one another like happy people do, and I listened keenly, if indirectly, delighted by the celebration and the extended family's vocal, almost-musical contentment. Raucous bark or quiet giggle, each individual echoed the holiday gathering's warmth and friendship, and those carefree sounds invaded my spirit like the beating of live drums or sunshine after rain. I desperately wanted to be part of Emily's family. Desperately, because a heartbreaking, physical connection to these people enveloped me more completely with every passing second. Heartbreaking, because I quickly understood Emily wanted no such thing.

This night of my impolite awakening was Christmas Eve. Twenty-one people had been invited for dinner at the Soria's—Mama and Papi to Emily—and the acceptance rate had been one-hundred percent. There were aunts, uncles and cousins aplenty, sure, but Mama had grown up in the neighborhood and many of her friends' holiday parties would be held the next day, on Christmas, not Christmas Eve. So tonight, besides the family, six old friends had also chosen to share the evening with Mama and Papi.

We dined at a fifteen-foot-long, flattened-oval table with a card-table annex that extended the party from the Soria's dining room into their small parlor, blocking direct travel between the two rooms. Guests traveled around through the kitchen. The dining surface needed two red tablecloths, one embroidered with green holly branches, the other with forest-green ribbons. They almost matched. The Christmas-pattern china featured bright toys, boxed presents and decorated Christmas trees. Red-glass water goblets matched the color of the tablecloths, and white candles ringed by pine cones acted as centerpieces.

As her dinner table suggested, Mama Soria loved Christmas, and her seventy-five-year-old, two-bedroom framed house was decorated like a Manhattan department store. A string of colored electric lights had replaced the dining room chandelier, and another set of lights hung above the kitchen stove. Three separate Christmas trees had been garnished with ornaments, the biggest with us in the dining area, another seven-foot tree in the living room, and a third, slightly shorter one in the den where she and Papi watched television. Wreaths and ornaments carpeted every mantel, bookcase and table. Angels, Santa Clauses or toy soldiers protected the open corners of her floors.

Everyone had been eating five minutes or so when Emily groaned and grabbed her tummy. Her salad fork clattered against the china. I felt no surprise that Emily showed everyone her pain. What amazed me, she'd waited so long. See, I knew what bothered her. And how much the pain hurt.

"Are you all right?" Papi said. The professional auto mechanic sat two chairs away and hadn't whispered, so at least half of the dinner table's warm, happy chatter died. A sense of concern clouded the air like fog. Family and friends waited for Emily's answer—waited to hear if the night's celebration might be over, I suppose.

"My stomach hurts," Emily said. "I think it's my appendix."

Mama reached for her seventeen-year-old daughter's hand and squeezed it. Papi stretched around Mama to palm his daughter's forehead. "You do not have a fever."

"Maybe you should lie down," Mama said.

"Go to the emergency room," Abuelita said.

Abuelita was the family nickname for Mama's Italian-born mother, Angelina Pescara, and a name for Italian grandmothers everywhere. She'd survived this harsh world for eighty-nine years, stood five-foot-two in heels, and still lived by herself in a condo. A real sparkler in dangling earrings and bunches of silver bracelets, Abuelita owned enough costume jewelry to stock a mall.

Emily excused herself and went into the TV room to stretch out on the old sofa where Papi monitored Major League Baseball. She tried to rest, relaxing her muscles and mind, visualizing a handsome young man named Billy, flooding me with images and stories about her teenage crush—and apparently my father. Her romantic meditation techniques couldn't work on her pain, of course, and when Emily returned to the dinner table minutes later, in tears, announcing the need for a hospital emergency room visit, a bite of shrimp halted inches from Abuelita's fire-engine red lips.

"I told you," she said.

Emily cried all the way to Riverside General's emergency room. The pain bore in and frightened her, or the realization of what was about to happen bubbled up from her subconscious. On some level, she must have known, and her sadness about that undeniable truth cut me as well. Though I was both astounded and excited by the gigabits of information Emily had been feeding me, the incredible knowledge and memories I gained each passing second, what should have been a happy day was not.

Though her voice remained calm, Mama gripped the car's steering wheel with white knuckles. "Where exactly does it hurt, Emily? Where's the pain?"

"My stomach."

Her whining voice sliced my gut. She acted so miserable.

"High up or down low?"

"Both."

"Did you eat anything unusual last night or this morning?"

"Just drive, okay Mom? Let's make sure we get there."

"I'm driving perfectly fine."

The bright red lights of Riverside General's emergency pull-in area beckoned from less than two miles away, so Mama's car arrived quickly into the crimson glow. Except for the truck-size, electric EMERGENCY sign, the hospital was old, cold and scary, a complex of chipped cement and cracked brick buildings stuffed with a century of disease.

Inside the ER, windowless walls had been painted olive green, but antiseptics, floor wax and dark pigment couldn't mask the savage, underlying scent of body fluids and decay. Sickness and pain loitered in the air.

Emily and I perched near a suffering old man in a suit coat and ragged blue jeans several sizes too large while Mama approached the admissions counter, pulling insurance cards, identification and credit cards from her purse, anticipating one of the two nurses enjoying a conversation ten feet away would come to greet her. Neither appeared to notice her presence, and seconds ticked by. A minute. Another nurse pushed an occupied stretcher through the waiting room. The horizontal, moaning patient seemed a stark warning to those awaiting treatment.

The old man's whimpering unsettled both Emily and me, and I wished someone would help him. His distress grated on my skin like a carpenter's file, I wanted so much to ease the torment for him. I decided to try, concentrating on the terrible anguish I heard, trying to soothe him with my thoughts. Crazy idea, I knew, but after a few minutes passed, he seemed to quiet a little. Positive vibes can never hurt.

In perfect juxtaposition to the man's returning calm, Mama geared up for an outburst. After four minutes of being ignored, she rapped the counter with her knuckles, then spoke to the nurse with sharp but quiet words. Emily and I couldn't hear. The reception nurse was taller and heavier than Mama, and by pushing her nose within an inch of Mama's, she appeared anything but intimidated. She raised her voice, too, as we heard exactly what

4

she said to Mama next, the nurse pointing while she spoke: "Go sit by your dish."

Mama's face darkened. "My daughter's appendix is bursting and you make a joke? Dr. Raymond is a personal friend of this family. My husband plays softball with him. If this goes badly with my daughter because you—"

Emily picked that instant to vomit, a quick spill onto the emergency room floor. Mostly white wine, the mess also contained chunks of something I couldn't identify. Shrimp or clams? Funny I'd forgotten which, since for the first few minutes of my awareness that night, I believed I *was* Emily, or rather I'd believed we were the same person. Sure there was her and there was me, but there was nothing else, so I thought we were one. Over the past hour or so, I'd been force-fed her thoughts, her memories, her moods, likes and dislikes. And then earlier tonight at that incredible, galvanizing Christmas Eve dinner, I came alive with personal, private desires. I'd become aware of Emily's connection to the joy and fulfillment in that magnificent, loving family, and I wanted that love and security, too.

I understood mine was in jeopardy.

I'm not sure if Emily upchucking her pre-dinner snacks was the catalyst. Maybe Mama's mention of hospital Chief of Staff Dr. Raymond pulled the trigger. Whichever or whatever, that tough-talking, big-shouldered nurse asked a nurse with glasses to telephone a janitor, then emerged from behind her fortress. She snagged a stethoscope on the way out and marched directly to Emily.

"What are you doing?" Mama said.

The nurse kneeled beside Emily and placed the listening end of her stethoscope against Emily's chest. "I'm attending to your daughter. Hush and let me listen."

The chrome stethoscope moved onto Emily's abdomen and lingered.

"Your daughter doesn't have appendicitis," the nurse said.

"What's the matter with her?"

"Nothing's the matter, I don't believe. But there are *two* heartbeats."

"What?" Mama said.

"She's going to be a mother."

Mama gasped. "She's pregnant?"

The nurse stood. "Not pregnant. In labor. About to deliver her child. When did your water break, honey?"

Emily screamed "no,' the word wailing down a hallway and echoing back. Her face contorted, squeezing tears from her eyes.

"What?" Mama said.

That night, I think *what* was her favorite word.

The nurse shrugged and headed back to her fort. "Let's find out if there's a bed in delivery."

Mama leaned over a sobbing Emily. "How could you not know you were pregnant? How is that possible?"

Emily gasped for breath. "Do I look pregnant?"

Mama shook her head. "Not really. Not even overweight. Although that blouse is loose. But you didn't notice you stopped having periods?"

"I *did* have periods. Two this summer."

"Emily, there's no way."

Emily bellowed. Her body shook. "I *did*. Two. I've always been spotty."

"There's no way."

Mama and Emily's words dynamited my world. They'd talked about me as if I were a terrible or frightening thing, something they didn't want. How could I be bad? Why wouldn't Emily want a new baby girl? A smart and happy baby girl. I understood I didn't know everything about being a person yet. Heck, I was still in in the process of being born. Also, I recognized Emily to be childish in many ways. Too young to be a good mother. Self-absorbed. Still, her crying about my birth made me feel awful—like trash. Lonely and afraid. I knew by then she'd been hiding me, pretending I didn't exist, but why wouldn't Emily love me when I showed up? Her own daughter? I wanted to be part of the Soria family, attend happy dinners like the one earlier that night. But Emily and Mama made me think and feel I might get dumped.

"Who's the father?" Mama asked.

By this time Emily and I rode a stretcher headed for the hospital maternity ward and an unoccupied delivery room. Like a pitcher's best fastball, I was moving more ways than one.

Mama scurried to keep up. "Come on. Who?"

Her voice told me she cared what might happen. Both to her daughter and to me.

"Billy," Emily said. "Billy Wallace is the father."

"Not that musician, the druggie who left school?"

TWO

Talking to Emily and Mama in the delivery suite, a nurse used the term *cryptic pregnancy*. That made me worry my current arrival had something to do with death. Bodies in vaults. Was someone going to die? Mama must have thought the same thing because she came out and asked questions, made the nurse explain: Both English words *crypt* and *cryptic* came from the Greek *kruptos*, meaning hidden, which made a bunch of sense to me. Nobody had entertained the *idea* I might be inside Emily for nine months.

Now that's hidden.

Turned out that particular delivery nurse knew all kinds of statistics, like one in every four-hundred pregnant women don't discover there's a baby growing inside them until the child is twenty weeks old—the cutoff in determining if your pregnancy is cryptic or not. But the medical-school enrolled nurse said only a handful of pregnant women are like Emily; that is, they go to the hospital with pain and get the surprise of their life by delivering a child. Using Emily's least-favorite math term, decimals, the number would be 0.0004 percent of all U.S. births. About fifteen hundred surprise babies a year.

But the nurse said Emily was even more special by having displayed almost no symptoms. Most cryptically pregnant women don't show much because they're heavy, have health problems, or carry an odd-ball gene. Stress can be a factor and so can denial, the nurse explained. The emotional combination, which I'm pretty sure was true in Emily's case, allowed some bigger-boned women to *not look* pregnant; that is, the expanding uterus can partially hide itself beneath the lowest rib.

Emily remained in disbelief as they wheeled us into a delivery room. The lights were soft and didn't glare in her eyes. The walls had been painted three different pastel colors. A giant fan stood guard over one end of the delivery table, a robotic monitor. Plenty of blinking electronics surrounded us, but most of the connections awaited me, the baby. A soft chair occupied one corner for my non-present daddy.

In fact, Emily had no theory where my daddy lived.

New nurses collected us from the people who'd wheeled us inside. The new team wore blue robes and blue paper hats, white masks over their noses and mouths. Emily's mind spun, dizzy from all the medical stuff. And she still clung to the hope I wasn't really there. Maybe the emergency room nurse and the doctor backup both had been mistaken. You'd think the truth would have sunken in by then, especially when the one nurse talked about the major dilation of Emily's cervix.

I'm not sure how big ten centimeters is, but Emily's passage-way into life was definitely not large enough to suit me. In fact, everything had been pushing on me for hours. I felt like toothpaste emerging from a tube. Painfully and slowly, like an inch per hour. And after the agony of compression, the waiting world reminded me of that Eskimo bath torture where you steam your pores wide open in the sweat lodge, then run outside and jump in freezing water. The contrast was absolute, like good and evil.

Refrigerated air chilled my wet skin and gravity pulled directly on my organs for the first time. My senses flipped as I flopped— tugged and pushed out head-first into a pair of rubber gloves. The new, heavier weight of my body made me certain the human hands would drop me. I wanted to cry but there was no air in my lungs. And later, after people poked me and stuck things in my nose and mouth, and I could breathe on my own and could have cried if I'd wanted, I didn't because the complaints would have done me no good. This was my new world and I might as well get used to it. Whatever would happen would happen. Nothing could change my discomfort, or Emily's. A whole world filled with cold air instead of warm fluid probably meant irritation for the rest of my life. Maybe that's what life was really about—trying to reclaim the safety and comfort you previously enjoyed inside a womb.

While I dealt with my new experiences, Emily's physical pain eased. Since my birth began, I'd been able to monitor her senses through our mutually connective umbilical cord. Even her feelings. Her fear of motherhood, for instance, had hummed through our connection like an electrical broadcast. Even after being detached and on my own I could feel those frightened vibrations. Emily's fear of raising me—her panic at being a mother—lived in the air like an advancing lightning storm. I reminded myself how young she was, how scared. But I could only see her distress over my birth as rejection. Her alarm was impossible not to take personally.

If Emily didn't want to be my mother, what did that predict for my future? I'd never attend another one of those happy Christmas Eve dinners, and that was crapola. You don't have to be around long to understand the world is a frightening place, that life includes situations you have no control over, that anything can happen. Everybody needs friends and a family.

Questions rolled around in my head like scared settlers circling their covered wagons. What if Emily didn't take me home? Who would adopt me? Where would I go? Were nice families still adopting babies in this bad economy? I didn't want to be thrown out into a chilly, windy world all alone.

After a while, they let Mama inside Emily's delivery room, and Hope walked inside with her. Emily had barely glanced at me, only confusion and fear on her face. She'd refused to hold me beside her in bed and the nurses glanced knowingly at one another. All my fears seemed to have come true—until Mama walked in and looked at me. A warm light bounced back and forth between us and a connection stirred and wired itself inside me. Anyone could tell Mama stared at a thing she loved. Me. Something special.

The nurses saw. They let Mama hold me.

I used my gaze and my toothless smile to give back Mama all the love I could feel coming from her, as if love traveled on the light waves between peoples' eyes. Like a steady flashbulb I spilled my love, hot and bright, and I realized there existed inside me untapped mines of the stuff. Plenty of love. I must have inherited a big heart from this lady holding me, Mama, my grandmother.

Clutching me in her arms, Mama stared at Emily. "You have a responsibility to this child."

Both nurses glanced away, perhaps embarrassed by hearing what they'd wanted to say. But from the hospital bed, Emily rolled her brown eyes in a circle. Her lips mouthed the word *responsibility* in exaggerated fashion. Sarcastic and mean. She'd acted like a twelve-year-old. Mimicking her own mother.

"You created this life," Mama said. "This little girl is counting on you."

Was I? By then, I sort of expected Emily to ditch me. Her feelings about me seemed clear. Denying my existence. Crying over my birth. Refusing to hold me. The only thing she could have added to make me suffer worse? Maybe squeezing me into a ball and tossing me into the green trash can like the Name Form one of the nurses had given her.

Mama pleaded and begged for more than an hour, but Emily wouldn't hold me or agree to fill out new papers with a name for me. Eventually, Emily pulled the bedcovers over her head and pretended to sing to herself. Mama had gone outside twice to call Papi, tell her husband what had been going on at the hospital, but at four o'clock in the morning, Mama gave up and said she had to go home.

As soon as Mama left, the nurses tried again to entice Emily to hold me, talking about how good I smelled, how smart and happy a baby I was, but Emily said she was too tired and needed sleep. They pressed her on a name for the baby, too, but Emily was still refusing as I drifted off to sleep.

At some point the nurses wrapped me in warm dry blankets, placed me in a three-foot long plastic box and wheeled me to a room full of other newborn babies. I couldn't see anyone when I woke up again, and I cried I felt so alone. Unwanted. I guess at some point almost everyone judges themselves unloved. It's part of being human, I have a hunch. Sure seems a common theme in literature. But for me, the moment I woke up alone in the baby tank...well, that one topped all heartbreak scales and charts I could ever imagine. Emily didn't want to hold or even look at me. Neither my mother or my father—the people who created me—had any interest in caring for me. What circumstances could be worse for a newborn baby, an immobile blob of needy flesh, totally dependent on others for survival?

I cried worrying what would happen to me. Where would I end up? Who would take care of me? Why didn't I even have a name? I guess because of Christmas, the nurses sometimes called the boys Noel and us girls Noelle, which one of them did to me, but I hadn't seen Emily write anything on that second paper form.

Inside the hospital's glass baby tank, most of the other babies cried and fussed, too. Two boys screamed like banshees, the noise sharp. So sad and miserable. I couldn't see how screaming accomplished much. I figured such tantrums might make the nurses nervous or angry. When I cried, I cried quietly.

Lonely hours passed, and the glass baby box grew darker. Little green lights glowed here and there, but the place became as black as a movie theater. Maybe the nurses needed an hour or two of sleep. Hours earlier I had existed as part of something much bigger—a family celebrating an annual holiday. We weren't by ourselves, not individual entities. We were a team, a tribe, a collection of souls helping each other on the same journey, celebrating our closeness in a troubling, difficult world. And then a tiny slice of time later, there I was, all alone and frightened in the dark. No one but silhouetted strangers in uniform.

I told myself not to be angry at Emily. More than anything, I believed Emily was in shock that she'd delivered a baby. Scared, worried, embarrassed, thinking about herself mostly, for sure. But shocked would be the biggest thing. How the crapola—one of Emily's favorite words—did I happen? Only shock explained why she could be so mean when Emily was not a mean person. The opposite. She possessed rare intelligence and earned all A grades in school without working too hard. She had a shot this year at the Senior Honor Society, *Los Renombrados*. But she hadn't known she was pregnant, and she hadn't seen a doctor after her periods had gotten super spotty, then disappeared. Was she stupid or stubborn?

I knew her well enough to know Emily seriously feared raising me, so maybe her own self-preservation had turned up the dial on denial. She'd almost panicked being wheeled into delivery, imagining being my mother. She plainly hadn't wanted the job. She didn't want to nurse a baby, change dirty pants—even disposable paper ones—or teach a child anything about life. Those ideas terrified her. How could she ever be as good a parent as Mama?

In that same way, her feelings about raising babies echoed her mixed feelings toward independence. At seventeen, part of Emily wanted to be on her own, living her own life, not the life her parents managed for her. At the same time, like many seventeen-year-olds, Emily had become well aware of her shortcomings in the prepared-adult department. She changed her mind a lot and tended to get over-emotional. She cried at night sometimes without knowing why. How could she be a smart grown-up, capable of taking care of her own life, if she kept making giant mistakes about herself and her feelings? How could she be an adult if she wasn't smart and wise like her mother? Emily worried about living a life on her own, away from the safety of Mama's wisdom.

When I thought about her, I felt sorry for Emily, not angry.

Daylight streamed in the hospital windows, warming my spirits. Only darkness had existed while being born: Never before had I personally witnessed the startling difference between night and day. My mother had passed me libraries of information during birth, including much about sunsets and sunrise, mentions from the movies she'd seen and the books she'd read. But until that first morning in the hospital, I'd only imagined the sun through Emily's head.

Spilling out last night into the hospital lights had been a bombshell surprise. Seeing the different shapes of people and things with my own eyes. But somehow this first sunrise was an even bigger event, perhaps a kind of spiritual awakening. Where would we humans be without the warmth and illumination of sunlight?

The new natural warmth gave me hope again, and I couldn't help but wonder if the Egyptians, Aztecs and a hundred other ancient peoples had chosen the perfect representation of God when they worshipped the sun. With our star's toasty sunshine on my face, I could dream again Emily would change her mind about giving me away. My skin tingled.

The renewed optimism didn't last long.

One of the boy newborns screamed, and another one quickly joined in. That got the nurses busy changing all our pants, and as she strapped up my bottom again in clean paper, the nurse said, "Can you believe this Soria girl's mother didn't ask about her all night? A baby like this?"

Crapola. That warm sunny feeling slipped away. In fact, I cried. Emily had convinced herself for nine months she wasn't really pregnant. She was only seventeen and had no husband. My birth was going to be a big hassle, a real problem with her social life. She'd tell Mama today to have me adopted. I knew what was in her mind.

One of the baby tank nurses tried to sooth me. My quiet sobs had caught her attention while she'd changed me. Her name was Betty. "Don't feel so bad, little one. Two other girls are headed for adoption as well. It's a nasty world you've been born into. But you'll survive. You might be the prettiest, smartest baby I've ever seen."

THREE

Morning visiting hours arrived, the maternity department's double doors separated and a rush of humanity gathered outside the baby tank to stare at us inmates. I was thrilled to see a decent-size group focused on me. I recognized Mama, Papi and their son Phillip—Emily's brother—plus a girlfriend of Emily's, Demyan, a pink-haired rebel who glared like a snake, her beady eyes unblinking, her pierced tongue nervously tasting the air.

Okay, maybe I imagined the part about her sampling the air, but Demyan definitely had a stainless steel stud through her tongue. Yuk. Demyan also was the so-called friend who introduced Emily to cigarettes, tattoos, marijuana and cocaine, not to mention boys, unsupervised dance parties, condoms and the advantages of a quick hand-job. Kindly, Mama once said Demyan was not lady-like. If Mama had known but a percentage of Demyan's past actions and entertainment preferences, Mama would have chased Demyan from the house shouting *puttana*.

Yes, I knew by then there was something special about me, though perhaps not as exceptional as some people might have thought. All babies understand way more than grown-ups imagine. Basic emotions are not taught, they're instinctive, so babies suffer many human feelings from the first moment we're born. Love and fear, mainly, the fear whenever our environment is disrupted. But for some of us—well, me anyway, and probably many others to some degree—the umbilical cord had fed me Emily's emotions and thoughts during the hours I was being born, the flood of information tagging along on her body's regular supply of oxygen and nourishment. The mental connection had barely faded since the doctor cut the cord, too. I'd continued to hear most of Emily's thoughts, and still drew memories of the books she'd read and shows she'd watched.

Maybe that *is* pretty special. I don't know. It does seem weird that I know more world history than Uncle Phillip's teacher. But honestly, I think the only thing special about me, I loved words. My head was full of them. Mostly Emily's, but also from characters in the books she'd read and the films she'd watched. Her friends and other people she talked to. So many different kinds of words. The quick, bombastic sentences of private eye novels. Gumshoes, thirty-eight specials and mouthpieces. The long, tangled sentences of nineteenth century storytellers, both male and female, published monthly, and most tellingly, paid by the word. Words like soothsayer, urchins and graveyard haunts. About the only novels Emily didn't enjoy were books that had won big international prizes. They seemed much alike to her, stories of women growing up in the most rural and desperate places, women with no connection to Emily's world. Me, I liked hearing about those foreign lands, strange domains where life and death hovered near a violent surface, where a decent meal and a night's sleep were rare, treasured events. Not Emily. My access to those stories was limited.

I learned so many words so fast, digging into her memory for every expression she'd heard or read, all in a matter of hours, my personal thoughts were arriving in eclectic and jumbled fashion as well. I'd tried to hold onto every single phrase I'd run across because, as far as information and knowledge go, I understood words were the tools *and* building blocks. But I needed to issue a warning, mention my brain was handling all kinds of crapola— probably too much, too soon. I could fly off on a tangent.

So visiting hours had limits and rules, meaning the nurses

soon waved off the gawking visitors and one-by-one wheeled the babies into individual patient rooms off the main circular maternity nurses station. The set-up reminded me of spokes off a wheel. Slips of paper and even my picture had been taped above me inside the plastic bassinette, and the nurses carefully checked to make sure they had the right child before delivering me to Emily.

Once more a nurse tried to make Emily cuddle me. The maternity staff apparently had a routine for reluctant moms, and that knowledge helped me cope a little with Emily's cold disregard. If this motherly rejection thing happened a lot, as the nurses' actions suggested, many reluctant mothers changed their mind once they held their child in their arms.

In some new-thinking places, I'd overhead, moms didn't have the option of sleeping away from their newborns. Baby tanks were banned so the mothers better bonded with their babies. At least that's what those new-thinkers believed. And while that set-up sounded especially good to me just then, my hospital still believed moms were super tired after giving birth to half a dozen pounds of joy. They needed sleep and rest.

Mama, Papi, Phillip and Demyan filed into Emily's private room minutes behind the nurse and me. They heard Emily refuse to hold me as they scrunched in a corner near the foot of Emily's bed. Demyan positioned herself closer to Emily, blocking light from the window. Demyan's spiked pink hair threw a jagged shadow across my plastic bassinette.

The nurse lifted me, cradled me and showed me up close to Mama and Papi. I immediately stopped crying and smiled like a circus clown. If you want people to like you in this world, be a bumper-sticker for love, make them heart you. Be open, kind and honest. Think about corporate balance sheets—be an asset to people, not a liability. And since all I had to give others was a smile, I gave Emily's mom and dad—the people I hoped would be my family—the biggest, best smile I could manage. Times were tough all over America. I offered the Sorias every reason possible to take me in.

Emily's parents appeared split on the issue. Mama had everything correct immediately, perceiving with one examination last night that I was a wonderful child—pretty, intelligent and good-natured. She again asked to hold me in her arms. Papi acted cold and stand-offish, though. He didn't speak the word I knew to be on his mind, but the message flashed in his eyes. Illegitimate was not the term he'd used.

I saw something else in his gaze I found encouraging, though. He deeply loved Mama. Maybe I didn't need to worry much about his opposition. He'd come around if Emily and Mama could be convinced to take me home. Besides, he was a man. He'd spend more time watching sports than taking care of me.

When Mama finally handed me back, the nurse again extended me to Emily. If nothing else, the green-clad nurses were persistent warriors for familial love. But a little, I felt like a tray of stale donuts being passed around. Only Mama wanted one and maybe she was being polite. Emily once more refused to touch me. She became teary-eyed pushing me away. "I don't want to be a mother," she said. "I'm practically a child myself."

How did that make me feel? Imagine a deer stealing quietly through the forest when a hunter's arrow pierces her flesh, shocking her organs into failure. Yes, I'd known Emily had acted all along as if she didn't want me. Convincing herself I didn't exist. Thinking of me as a sore appendix. Crying at my birth. Refusing to hold me. But until the moment when she spoke the words out loud, described her true feelings to her own mother...well, I'd held out hope. The nurses knew mothers often changed their minds. Why shouldn't Emily? In my gut, I'd calculated the odds and thought maybe, possibly, she'd eventually want me. The determination in her voice, however, and those simple words 'I don't want to be a mother' ended that dream. I knew what came next.

"You'd give her up for adoption?" Mama said.

"What else can I do? I'm seventeen. I don't have a job, a

husband or a place to live except for your house."

"Our daughter is usually full of *refritos*," Papi said, "but I think not this time. Emily is making sense. You and I are way too old to raise a baby."

"Speak for yourself," Mama said. "And that's no way to talk to your daughter. Especially now."

Papi grunted. Mama and Papi seemed like totally different people in many ways, Italy versus Mexico, but neither one liked to give up on an important argument.

"We've raised two kids," she said. "We can help raise another one."

He frowned at Emily. "Help? Emily has little or no interest in taking care of her child. I believe it would be obvious to most people that Emily cannot take care of herself."

"Stop it," Mama said.

Emily lifted her chin. "Papi's right. The baby would be better off with someone who wants children."

My body shook, top to bottom and side to side. When the convulsion stopped, I'd lost focus on that asset-vs.-liability thing. I sobbed and sobbed. The nurse held off putting me back in the bassinette, and cuddled me, but the hurt inside wouldn't let me gather command.

I'd known her feelings were coming, the exact words from Emily's mouth even expected. But once again, the actual, physical sound of them drove home her emotion, her fear of raising me, and my spirit understood exactly how badly my mother wanted to give me away.

And Papi kept chiming in against me. Mama joined me in the sobbing, my grandmother bursting into tears like a teenager. Like me.

Demyan shifted, positioning herself to the side of Emily's parents so Mama and Papi couldn't see her face. I could. When Emily glanced at her pink-haired friend, Demyan rolled her eyes clownishly when Mama spoke—like Mama ranked as the dumbest person ever. The eye-rolling thing must have been another wonderful talent Demyan had taught Emily.

In my mind, Demyan was worse than young and foolish, or even stupid. There was no shine or light in her eyes, no friendship offered, not even the fake kind a salesman can throw around. Her gaze registered as blank, a cypher that concentrated on a distant place no one else could see.

As if she'd heard me think, Demyan drifted closer to my bassinette. She stared, my face arousing a curiosity in her, apparently. She examined the shape of my mouth, nose and ears, as if she wanted to remember what I looked like. Scary coming from Demyan, whose pink hair rose from her scalp like two rows of six-inch nails. She wore clingy jeans and a black, short-sleeved T-shirt showing a bicolored, crossbones tattoo on each forearm. These days, wild dress didn't make her evil. But I sure didn't like that blank squint in her eyes.

I shifted my gaze to Emily's brother, Phillip. He'd shuffled closer to me as well and located himself beside Demyan for a better look. Only fifteen, Phillip was already taller than most grown men. About six-five. When Phillip smiled at me, I sensed a concern his school pals would tease him about being uncle to an illegitimate baby.

Trying to stop my crying, Mama removed me from the nurse's arms. With the gentle hands of an angel, she again held me tightly against her breast. Her warmth soothed the pain inside me. Her gaze and her strong, loving heartbeat halted my distress.

"Oh, Emily," Mama said. "This little girl is our flesh and blood. She belongs to us."

Mama loved me, a realization that not only quieted my suffering, but also recalled for me the common caring I'd experienced the previous night at dinner—that secure, tribal sensation of being with people who loved and took care of each other.

Emily sniffed and rocked her head. Demyan spun her eyes.

I must have fallen asleep in Mama's welcoming arms because I woke up later confused, inside the rolling plastic bassinette still parked beside Emily's hospital bed. A chill had unsettled me when I'd opened my eyes, and the coldness remained on my skin although two thick blankets covered me.

Phillip, Mama and Papi had gone. So had the nurses. Only Demyan's tinny voice droned on and on about something that, in my drowsiness, I didn't at first understand. What was the *it* she kept telling Emily to get rid of? Not until Demyan used the word *adoption* while standing over my bassinette, staring into my wakening eyes, did I realize she'd been talking about me the whole time. Probably why I felt cold, too. What kind of person speaks like that about another person? It? Demyan Kinsky claimed to be of Russian descent, but I think her soul hatched from ancient living rocks on the black side of the moon. She definitely gave me the creepolas. Maybe the crapolas, too. I wish Emily wouldn't listen to her so much.

"You're seventeen years old," Demyan said. "Motherhood is the end of your life. You can't bring that baby home. Who'll want to go out with you if you have a kid? Nobody, that's who. You can forget having dates for the rest of your boring life. You need to lace up, girl. Do not listen to your mother."

Emily cried and didn't answer although I knew she loved to party. Demyan was probably right that Emily becoming a mother would end her romantic involvements for a while. Emily was seventeen and selfish. There was nothing I could do. Was there?

Later, headed back toward the baby tank in my plastic bassinette, another idea popped into my head—maybe I'd be better off adopted. At least then I would be raised by a mother and a father, parents who wanted me. *Really* wanted me, people who would go through difficult adoption proceedings, hire lawyers, spend time and money to have me forever change their lives. Isn't that love? It's something, sure. But maybe not the same as being raised and loved by your natural and genetically matched mother and father.

My gut wrenched and I wondered what happened to nature in Emily's case. Young women and men were supposed to fall under the spell of natural hormones when they produced a child, bonding chemicals produced by organs and delivered to special brain receptors, all in effort to create strong protective instincts and fondness for their offspring. Like mama bear risking her life to feed and nourish her young. Or birds protecting their chicks in the nest.

Something had failed with Emily's hormones. Or maybe her receptors were just filled with pot.

I wanted to grow up, live and start my own family with Emily, Mama, Papi and Phillip close by, part of that larger family or tribe I'd sensed at Mama and Papi's Christmas Eve dinner. But if that possibility looked less and less likely, I needed an alternative.

What else was there but adoption?

Back in the baby tank for our scheduled feeding, much-needed clean pants and a mandatory rest period, even the boy's screeches quieted under the weight of a dark, gloomy naptime. Outside the hospital windows, blue-black squall clouds collected, and sleep invaded the nursery like impenetrable, horror-movie fog. Both of our baby tank nurses succumbed. Betty even snored. We newborns rested in our bassinettes, helpless as silverware.

A barely audible *tick-tick* made me search for the source, but the sound came from outside my view. Some of the outer glass reflected people or objects, especially if the person moved, and two ceiling mirrors peered down the hallway in both directions, their curved surfaces directed toward the baby tank's nurse station. I'd noticed them while I'd been wheeled around. There was much to see above my bassinette, in and out of the baby tank, but this particular ticking noise escaped me.

The sound grew louder. And closer. I couldn't imagine a cause, the vibration so insignificant yet oddly frightening to my body. Why was I on edge over unknown peeps or ticks? I was probably over reacting to the emotional events of the day. Like being born. Then again, perhaps I'd received a primal, instinctive warning about approaching danger.

Seconds later, a reflection on the baby tank front window showed up on one of the high mirrors focused on the hallway. Two seconds passed before I was totally sure of what I saw— two seconds before I recognized Emily's friend Demyan as the noise's source. The *tick-tick* sound came each time Demyan's steel-studded tongue double-struck the baby tank window.

FOUR

Emily had seen an old horror movie where the main character transformed into a werewolf. In her memory of that time, Emily had rubbed her forearms to rid herself of what she'd called goosebumps. I hadn't quite understood what she meant until Demyan's eyes stared back me in that high, round security mirror, her steel-tipped tongue creating another *tick-tick* noise against the baby tank glass. My skin crawled into miniature knots. Oh, yeah, I thought. Goosebumps.

Demyan's reflection grinned at me, as if she realized she'd scared me. Her previously cold and measuring eyes sparkled like polished glass. The dread crawling over me grew worse, unbearable, and I experienced a sense of doom I'd never imagined could exist. Fear was a common, if unpleasant, part of the human experience. But what Demyan had done to me hit harder and came across as unnatural, like knowing the mythical figure of Death itself had chosen me: I'd been transported into a play where the black-robed Grim Reaper openly stalked her next prey.

Emily had read a lot of weird books.

Demyan kept her glassy gaze on my bassinette while she edged along the hallway, brushing the baby tank windows with her fingertips as well as the occasional *tick-tick* with her tongue. Like kissing the glass. Weird and silly, maybe crazy—cray cray, like Emily's other friends say—but somehow Demyan's snake act totally charmed me. Like paralyzing nerve venom, her stare froze me speechless inside my bassinette. The perception of impending annihilation overwhelmed me, forced me to recognize my fate. Bound me to the inevitable end. I watched Demyan advance exactly like the mice at a snake farm watched the snake coming to eat them—transfixed. Demyan probably wouldn't bite me, though. I guessed she'd cover my nose and mouth so I couldn't breathe. She could use a blanket, or imagining Demyan the way I did, apply her hand.

She'd consider personal, skin-on-skin contact more entertaining.

Demyan paused at the nursery entrance and straightened, lifting her chin to stretch herself taller into the air like a stalking cobra. I imagined I heard each disk of her long spine click into place. Her spiked pink hair twisted left then right, Demyan checking the hall in both directions. She next surveyed every corner of the glass box nursery where she hoped to dine. Demyan did not want witnesses.

Okay, I know my descriptions sound over dramatic. I'm down with others not buying her evil intentions because there was no logical explanation why I judged her so wickedly motivated. But my fear and distaste were instinctive and so strongly focused, I could not ignore the warning. Demyan wanted somehow to harm me, if not actually murder me. I could smell her fear of me, her plots—a pungent odor, like pee. The young woman's selfish concern for herself, which she'd projected into a concern for Emily, wanted me out of Emily's life. I sensed there was even more to her feelings, another motive for her dislike, but I had no more time to consider.

Demyan's pink spikes darted inside the baby tank. My heart bumped wildly. Where were the baby nurses? I'd thought they were asleep, but I heard and saw nothing. How could we newborns be left alone in our glass prison while this demented, teenage creepola roamed freely among our bassinettes? I could hardly breathe as Demyan tip-toed up the main aisle, her eyes concentrated on my bassinette. Purpose haunted her quiet foot-falls. Each step vibrated on my taut skin.

I sucked in all the air my newly working lungs would hold, planning to emit a scream worthy of the helpless female victim in that horror movie Emily had watched. But I couldn't. I'd choked up. Invisible, assaulting hands surrounded my throat, and my wide open mouth turned dry as sand.

I lost sight of Demyan and held my breath to listen. An hour seemed to pass. Endless seconds, I suppose. Half a minute? Then the familiar *tick-tick* vibrated glass or steel directly behind me, near the top of my head. The creepy sound was so close— Demyan was so close—my whole body flexed as if I'd been shocked by electricity. My vision darkened at the edges. I must have been a second or two from passing out.

Where were those nurses?

Strong hands spun my bassinette in a fast half-circle, the wheels squealing as they raced over the tile. My weight shifted higher—toward the top of the bassinette—and at the same time rolled to one side. Cold plastic pressed against my scalp. I tried again to cry out, but fear still strangled me. I'd never been jostled like that.

My weight shifted the opposite way as the bassinette jerked toward the nursery's rear corner, away from the front spectators' window. Though I couldn't see her, I knew those strong hands dragging me away belonged to Demyan. There had been no one else around. She hadn't tried to smother me, as my imagination suggested, but there was still plenty of time.

At least fear and the galloping bassinette improved my blood flow. A pounding heart brought my darkened vision into better focus.

I needed to scream. My life felt in danger. Searching for the wind to produce a real wail, the bassinette stopped moving and those strong hands disappeared from my plastic container. Seconds later I saw a reflection of Demyan hurry outside the nursery. I was safe again. As my terror eased, my confusion peaked. I was thrilled to still be breathing, honestly, but why had Big Pink shifted me into the nursery's corner?

Two minutes later I understood. That's when Demyan and Emily strolled past the baby tank, shoulder to shoulder, laughing and heading for the EXIT sign. More than a passage outside, for Emily that doorway represented escape from parental responsibilities. Demyan had shifted me back into a corner so I'd be harder to spot and therefore easier to leave should Emily glance at the nursery on her way out. Demyan's preparations were unnecessary, however. Emily never peeked my way. She'd hustled out of there, dressed for the teenage spots again, in slim-fit jeans and a sequined, low-cut blouse. Her pal Demyan must have brought her fresh clothes.

Nothing new, I suppose. No additional information. Emily didn't want me. She'd left me there. My heart hissed flat like a spiked tire.

Returning to the maternity ward, one of the nurses—Betty, my favorite—smelled faintly of cigarette smoke, so I guessed she'd been outside on a smoke break while Demyan had shifted my bassinette. Before Betty noticed my empty spot in the rows of bassinettes, the other baby-tank nurse wandered back inside the glass as well. The two women stared at each other, both surprised, Betty maybe a little angry. Betty wore thick black eyebrows that pinched together like a vise.

"You told me I could go out for a smoke," Betty said.

"It's okay," Kayla said. "I wasn't gone two minutes. And Margaret said she'd keep an eye open."

Margaret must have been the name of the maternity-station nurse. The department's headquarters was a half-circle desktop of pale orange, across and down the hall maybe fifteen yards from the nursery entrance. Clutter on the orange desk partially obscured Margaret's view, as did racks of equipment and baby products stationed temporarily in the hall.

Betty wagged her head. "You know one of us always has to be here."

"I had a serious bathroom emergency."

That's when Betty noticed the hole in the regimented ranks of her nursery's plastic bassinettes. Her eyes bloomed. "Where's Noelle Soria?"

Kayla gasped, then found me and pointed. "There...in the corner."

Betty rushed to my side. "She's been moved. It wasn't you?"

"No."

Betty examined me. "She seems fine."

I squealed an agreement, although Demyan's ticking tongue still twisted my gut a little.

Kayla laid her palm on my forehead. "She's warm."

Worse than warm, I was hot. But those two nice nurses Betty and Kayla got my biggest, best smile. Demyan hadn't touched me. There was no need for medical attention. And I'd been way wrong about Demyan wanting to smother me. Why had I been so paranoid? The pink-haired creep had scared me plenty, though, yanking my bassinette around like that.

"She needs her diapers changed," Kayla said.

Demyan scared me plenty, like I said. And if the chance ever presented itself, getting even with Big Pink would scratch an intense itch.

No one came to see me in the baby tank all afternoon, and I couldn't help but wonder again if adoption, though not my first choice, might be the smart one. A mom and dad who took the trouble and money to go through a strenuous legal and financial process would logically provide a better home than a teenage mother who'd ditched me.

Right?

Speaking of ditched, I overheard the nurses talking later about abandonment, the harsh word carrying legal definitions

and requiring hospital paperwork. I didn't understand everything they said at first, but apparently the term applied to my
mother's actions—leaving me alone at the hospital. Moms are
allowed to leave their babies behind if they can't afford them or
don't know how they're going to raise a baby. So-called *safe
haven laws* exist in all fifty states, much legislation having
followed notorious cases in the 1990s, including two children
dumped in the trash. Ditching me at the hospital wasn't a crime.
But apparently there would be consequences.

Mama showed up at the hospital again late that evening. Visiting
hours were over, but the baby tank nurses Betty and Kayla not
only let Mama look at me, they suggested she hold me. What
wonderful moments those were, my grandmother's warmth and
tender words lighting that family fire again inside me. I had
never felt so loved.

"You are so beautiful," Mama said. "You might grow up to
be a movie star."

I wasn't sure I wanted to be an actress. So many had to
scream at monsters. But I smiled at Mama anyway.

"Oh, you agree, huh?"

I expanded my smile to a wide, toothless grin.

Mama laughed. "You're definitely an actor."

I giggled, Mama laughed harder, and Betty the smoking
nurse came over to find out what was so funny. I could smell
hints of tobacco as she leaned in close to Mama and stared at
me for a long moment. Betty's eyes were a gorgeous, pale
blue—like steely winter skies.

"Your granddaughter is unbelievably intelligent," Betty said.
"I've never seen a newborn so aware of her surroundings."

"She does seem to be paying attention, doesn't she?" Mama
said. "None of my children were like this."

"I've worked with newborns for eight years. She's really
special."

Mama sobbed and squeezed me in her arms, but she hid her face so I wouldn't see her cry.

"What's wrong?" Betty said.

Mama slipped me into my bassinette. I immediately missed the warmth of her. The caring. "My daughter's seventeen and doesn't think she's capable of raising a child. I'm sure it's more about her social life, her lack of responsibility. But she's decided to put my granddaughter up for adoption."

Betty nodded. "We noticed she'd left without her child. We had to record the time."

"What do you mean, record?"

"Write it down. Log it. The state's child services agency requires us to document the time of abandonment."

"Abandonment? What a terrible word."

Betty nodded toward me. "Imagine what she thinks of it."

Mama stared at me in the bassinette and choked, her throat inhabited by a hamster, the flesh shifting and bulging as if something unswallowable wiggled inside. Poor Mama. The idea of leaving me behind was too much. Her next words burst like water through a broken dam. "If my daughter gives this child away, I will never live another happy day."

Betty stared at me. "This little Noelle is so smart and beautiful."

I enjoyed the compliments, but the discussion hardly lifted my spirits. My future at the adoption market seemed no longer in doubt, but every time I heard another confirmation, the rip in my heart muscle grew wider and deeper.

The rainwater on Mama's clothes must have also gotten into her eyes. She sniffed. "I'll raise her by myself if I have to. She's my flesh and blood. I will not abandon her. I swear I would never smile again."

Mama sobbed. Betty found tissues in the desk drawer and offered them, but the nurse's act of kindness or concern triggered Mama's previously rubbery face to set like stone. She refused the tissues, stretched a hand deep into a carry bag for her cell phone. Pressing buttons, my grandmother marched out of the nursery and through the wide double doors marked EXIT.

If my hunch was right, Emily was about to receive an emotional phone call.

Was there still hope for me?

FIVE

Nurse Betty wheeled me to my regular slot on the baby tank's main aisle, closer to the outside hallway. The other newborns slept or were at least quiet, but pained and troubled voices drifted in from private rooms close by, and I found renewed hope difficult. Mama might change a seventeen-year-old daughter's mind, but from what I knew and things I'd seen, a heartfelt turnaround in Emily appeared unlikely. Would Emily be a good mother because Mama convinced her to keep me? Adoption might offer a better life.

Not that Emily was a bad person. Quite the contrary. She was kind to friends and strangers alike, loved animals, enjoyed reading and learning about the world, and kept conscientious care of her charges when babysitting for the neighbors. She also helped Mama and Papi cook and clean. But no way Emily wanted to be a mother. Not now. She thought she wanted a career. Naturally artistic, Emily had several talents, including painting and drawing, poetry, and her favorite—music. Her voice produced notes on time and in perfect pitch, and her illustrations with pen and paper had been sold to online magazines. Lately though, most of her artwork involved big penciled hearts with Billy Wallace's initials inside.

Mama reappeared in the nursery twenty minutes later, her hair damp and the shoulders of her coat and the tops of her walking sneakers soaked. Adding to the determination in her eyes, Mama's new wet and wild appearance produced an image of quiet-but-aggressive resolve—like a special forces soldier.

"Is she asleep?" Mama asked.

"Go look," Betty said.

Instinctively, I squealed happily to forego any doubt, and both Mama and the nurse laughed. The previously mentioned, asset-vs.-liability thing must have been hard at work inside me. Be funny, that instinct told me, and the resulting laughter from the two women made me happier. Also improving my mood was the expression of resolve and success on Mama's face. I figured she'd talked Emily into coming back. Apparently, hope was something I couldn't let go of.

Mama smiled as she ambled to my bassinette. Her soft hands pulled me to her chest. Our hearts beat together.

"Hi there, beautiful girl," Mama said. "Were you talking to us just then?"

I grinned at her. What a wonderful, loving woman Mama Soria was. I stared happily into her easy brown eyes, the tan iris flecked with darker, soft-edged spots. Like chocolate-chip cookies still warm from the oven, she smelled of toasted sugar.

"Oh, you're just such a charmer...aren't you?" she said.

Mama was smart, too. She'd picked up right away on my asset-liability instincts. She knew what my good-natured actions were all about.

"Well, it's not enough that *I* want you," Mama said. "We have to make your mommy want you. And you're going to help me, little babe. I talked Emily into coming back to the hospital tonight, to sign out officially, and when she gets here, you're going to help me change her mind about adoption. Change her mind about *you*."

Funny how I'd thought of her as Emily all this time, not mommy. Was I doing something subconscious there? Maybe it was the idea I first had that Emily and I were one thing, maybe the same person. I used her name to help me differentiate.

"I know it doesn't sound easy," Mama said, "but I think it might be less complicated than we imagine. Maybe, darling, you just keep smiling like you did to me, show Emily how perceptive and good-natured you are, how much joy your love could bring her."

Obviously, Mama understood and believed completely in my balance sheet equation. Maybe that's the glue that keeps all families strong, all loving relationships working—helping each other. Being an asset.

"All your mom can think about right now is boys, boys, boys," Mama said. "How no boy will ever ask her out again if she has a baby at home to take care of."

I knew better than that. More likely Emily thought of Billy, Billy, Billy. But I definitely understood Mama's point.

"Our job, when she gets here, is to remind your mother that real love is what matters in this world. Without love, there is no real happiness, only meaningless days without someone to care about, someone to care about you. That's no life at all, is it baby?"

I wished Mama had understood Emily better. Love was important to Emily, too—but love for Billy, not a child. And she imagined Billy would love her more if she worked at her music, not at raising children and being a mother. Honestly, Emily was nuts about the guy, even though he'd never called after their one night together. I supposed his silence was under-standable considering what I think might have happened that night. Besides my conception that is. I can't imagine he'd ever want to see her again. But Emily needs to understand that fact and get over him. Instead, Emily spends half her evenings doodling on paper—making perfect red hearts with the initials BW inside.

As Demyan whispered to herself earlier, what a duster Emily could be.

"I'm telling you," Mama said, "there is no greater love in this world than a mother's natural love for her children. None. Boys and sex and marriage? Don't tell Papi, but that's how a woman acquires the love I'm talking about. A protective, nurturing mother's love is the foundation of virtually every species on the planet."

Sounds great Mama, except if a mother's love is so natural, what happened to Emily's? Our female ancestors produced children at younger ages than seventeen—for perhaps fifty- or a hundred-thousand years. If Emily's natural love wasn't there last night, this morning or even today, why and how would it show up tonight?

"You can't quit fighting," Mama said. "Your mother is a baby herself. She doesn't understand what she's giving up. She doesn't feel you yet."

No kidding.

"You have to show her the love, and keep showing her. She'll see the light. And you know I'm telling you the truth—love is more important than anything. Will you keep trying to change your mother's mind?"

I smiled. I didn't know what else to do.

"That's my babe," Mama said.

I wasn't totally sure what Mama expected me to do. How could I fight for anything? I couldn't talk to anybody. Sure, I could think and strategize, mentally carry out a plan if I had one, but the scheme couldn't involve physically moving anything, speaking out loud to people, or manipulating electronic devices. There were actions I could actually *do*, but I didn't think kicking the blankets off my feet, pooping or peeing would earn me Emily's love. In the right circumstances, perhaps natural functions might come in handy, but they were hardly an arsenal of activities with which to wage a war of survival. Although, I was a good kicker.

I supposed what Mama advocated was that I switch into full-charm mode, use my wiles and show Emily I could make her happy. But I figured Emily would probably like me better if I helped her locate Billy, or possibly a new musician-slash-boyfriend. Maybe I should troll the internet. If successful, I could write a book called Pimp Baby, make a million.

Emily, my teenage, single mother, returned to the hospital modeling her tight jeans and the scooped-neck silk blouse. Strutting her stuff, newly donned heels clicking on the maternity ward tile. Demyan and another, older woman walked inside with Emily, Big Pink dressed for a night out like my mother, the other woman holding a clipboard and wearing a drab green skirt and matching sweater.

Mama ignored Demyan and the green stranger to scowl at her daughter. A comment about Emily's dress seemed imminent, not only to me, but apparently to Emily as well—her eyes began to pinch. Two beats passed before Emily decided on diversion, not battle.

"This woman is some kind of baby cop," Emily said. "She wants to know why mine didn't have any pre-natal care."

"Could we talk privately, Mrs. Soria," the stranger said. "I'm not the police. I'm with the state's child services department. My name is Foster. Barbara Foster."

"My daughter didn't know she was pregnant," Mama said. "It happens all the time. There's even a reality TV show about it."

"Of course." The woman smiled in an unpleasant way, doll-like, displaying the insincerity of an overly professional public announcement. I guessed Barbara Foster to be thirty to thirty-five years old. Her dark red hair was set in short, tangled curls, a near-perfect halo around the circle of her face. Pale freckled skin; thick-framed glasses. She made me think of grammar school teachers. Or junior accountants. The air around Barbara Foster tasted of ink.

"Our concern is for the child," Foster said. "We are not here to point fingers, although if your daughter has abandoned her baby, that also becomes a state issue. Is that in fact what happened?"

"No, that is not what happened," Mama said. "My daughter is seventeen years old and under age. She—"

"Not as far as deciding about her child, Mrs. Soria."

Mama ignored her. "She left the hospital for a few hours without understanding the consequences. She and I need to talk. She's not giving up our own flesh and blood, no matter what her age is."

The woman consulted her clipboard. "That is interesting, certainly." Then she glanced at Emily. "But the mother told me very clearly and very directly a few minutes ago that she did not want to be a mother. Those are her own words. And by law this is her decision."

"We'll see about that," Mama said. "As I said Ms. Foster, Emily and I need to talk, and I don't think this family needs to be making important decisions this late at night. It's after nine. Why are you even here?"

Silence vacuumed the baby tank. The child services lady considered Mama, a stark assessment, from Mama's wet shoes to her wet hair, including a thirty-second, eye-to-eye tussle that reminded me of an old cowboy movie Emily had watched. If Foster's gaze revealed any judgment of Mama, I couldn't detect the assessment from my bassinette. The lady from child services could've made millions playing poker.

"There is a waiting room at the end of the hall," Foster said. "I suggest you and your daughter use that facility to sit down and have an honest, heart-to-heart talk. I will join you in a few minutes, after I speak to the maternity nurses and look through the child's medical charts. Does he have a name yet?"

"*It* is a *she*," Mama said.

"Sorry."

Mama dropped her sneer. "But no, there is no name yet."

"Her name's Noelle," Emily said.

Mama's forehead bunched. "What? When did you decide that?"

First I'd heard of it, too, except that's the name the nurses called all of us born on Christmas.

"The nurses were pushing me," Emily said. "I had to sign something."

Mama hustled Emily from the nursery. I watched them travel the hallway in the baby tank's high corner mirror, my grandmother and Emily parading toward the waiting area, or what Mama probably would have called the 'splaining department. Emily's body language indicated her participation was less than voluntary. Mama could have been dragging a live chicken to the chopping block.

The child services lady Barbara Foster spoke quietly after that with nurses Betty and Kayla, then paced beside my bassinette, snorting and sneezing like a horse as she read the medical charts the nurses had provided. Poor thing must have had allergies. Worse for me, Demyan stared at my bassinette the whole time, hovering at a distance from the nurses' station, Big Pink a quiet, unmoving shape, nearly invisible near one of the nursery's thick support beams.

Foster jotted notes on her clipboard for another five minutes, then joined Mama and Emily in that conference down the hall. I should have been invited to that pow-wow, as my future would be in the spotlight, but of course newborns have nothing to do and little to say in their own affairs. Kind of like American Vice Presidents.

Soon as Foster left, nurse Betty sought and received nurse Kayla's permission to go outside for a quick smoke. Kayla had been hesitant for a split second, but finally agreed. Demyan hadn't budged in all that time, nor taken her eyes off me, but ninety seconds after Betty disappeared from maternity, Demyan shifted her weight off the support beam.

Kayla had her head down, digging for something in a drawer.

"What's the matter, ma'am?" Demyan said.

Kayla's head snapped up. She slapped a hand to her chest. "Oh. You scared me."

"Sorry, but you look as if something's wrong."

39

I didn't how Demyan knew or saw anything about Kayla. I swear Big Pink hadn't seen anything but me in fifteen minutes. But the nurse laughed. "Every time my partner goes out for a smoke, I have to pee. I must have a bladder infection. I knew I should have used the bathroom first. You don't have an Advil, do you?"

Demyan shrugged. "No I don't, but why don't you just go pee. Just lace up and go get the job done. I'll stand guard, wait for you to come back. If one of these babies starts wailing, I'll come get you in the restroom."

Kayla shook her head. "I can't do that. It's against regulations to leave the babies unattended. And wrong. Dangerous. Betty said I could get fired."

"They're not unattended. I'm here. And I won't say anything. What are supposed to do, wet your pants?"

"It would be like two minutes. You sure?"

"Definitely," Demyan said. "I'd love to watch the babies."

"Okay, thanks. Two minutes."

To my ears, nurse Kayla's departure—the raspy sound of her diminishing footsteps—sounded like a horror-movie sound track. I lay helpless, alone in a room with Big Pink, protected only by other helpless blobs of newborn flesh. The blankets and bassinette trapped me on my back like a tortured prisoner. My pulse soared. What would Demyan do? She'd had plenty of time to plot, leaning against that pole, all still and silent, glaring at me.

SIX

One of the newborn boys shrieked like Tarzan as Demyan walked past his bassinette, a real howl. Obviously I wasn't the only baby who recognized Demyan as TROUBLE in all caps. Emily's pink-haired, tattooed pal belonged inside the same locked cupboard as sharp knives and loaded guns. She hurried on a straight line toward my bassinette.

There was no escape. Nothing to do but cry out, and I let it go, too, joining my new male friend four rows away by screeching at the moon. My primitive tones carried the shivering fear Demyan inspired, plus a little extra due to my somewhat overly dramatic nature. I remembered—and tried to recreate—what that skinny actress sounded like in that horror flick Emily had watched.

Before Demyan reached my bassinette, nine of the eleven babies in the tank had fallen in line, crying together in a gigantic wail, punishing their lungs, me and my new baby boy friend leading the acoustical attack. What a racket. My ears hurt. But I figured this Demyan situation called for a maximum alarm. What was she planning?

The noise worked. Demyan froze two yards from my bassinette. She hated the crying, or she was afraid the commotion would summon witnesses. Maybe both. Her cheeks and eyes contorted into a grotesque, pinched scowl, and her scary expression made our screaming that much easier. Yikes.

41

"What's going on in here?"

Fascinated by Demyan's unnerving approach, I hadn't noticed nurse Betty return from her smoke. She lingered now in the baby tank entrance, a frozen statue of reproach, hands on her hips, the boss lady of the newborns letting her presence work on us. Several babies shut down their crying, me included, and after a few private, nurse-patient consultations, Betty turned all the wails into silence.

Only after restoring order did nurse Betty turn to Demyan. "Where the hell is Kayla?"

"She had a bathroom emergency and asked me to watch for a few seconds," Demyan said.

"Again?"

"She mentioned a bladder infection."

Betty's head waggled side to side as she walked behind her desk station. The smell of tobacco had followed her inside the tank, only now reaching my bassinette. Someday—just wait—someday smokers will have to change clothes before coming back into the hospital. Maybe walk through a blast of ion-charged air.

"Everything was fine until this Soria baby started screaming," Demyan said. "The whole place just exploded."

Of course Demyan blamed me. She hid in the shadows with that spiked colored hair, weaseled a chance to be alone with us, then had the nerve to incriminate *me*. What was it about me that Emily's friend didn't like? Maybe that I hadn't liked her from the first minute I saw her? Okay, it's true I didn't like her pink hair and that I made fun of her when I called her Big Pink, but I believed the repellant was basic and instinctual, something in my blood.

A disturbance at the nursery entrance switched our attentions. Emily, Mama and Barbara Foster jostled and bumped arms and shoulders rushing through the portal. I was not surprised when Mama won the roller derby-like contest and gathered herself tall before the nurse's station.

"Is everything all right?" Mama said. "We heard the babies

crying."

Mama had asked the question of nurse Betty, but her gaze strayed to Demyan, and my grandmother's icy eyes and grim mouth said she knew that only Big Pink had been in the tank with us. I knew Mama to be such a kind loving person, with so much love, her black-dagger stare at Demyan unsettled me.

Demyan sneered back, but took a safer position beside her school chum Emily. Whatever Big Pink had planned, Mama had cancelled, and my grandmother was not finished.

Mama pushed herself between the two friends. Words and sentences exploded, bouncing off the window glass to create a slurring echo. Mama verbally leaped on Demyan for being so close to my bassinette. What had she been doing, Mama wanted to know, and why was Demyan all alone in the baby tank? What business could she have had with our family's new child? Demyan interrupted, noting repeatedly she wasn't Mama's child, anything she said or did was none of Mama's business. The smoking nurse Betty shouted over both of them, screaming at nurse Kayla, the one with the bladder infection. Kayla had returned but gotten stuck in the over-crowded access. And underneath the screaming mob—hiding in that special place where no one listens, but everyone talks—the child services lady Barbara Foster performed a short, low-pitched public service announcement: "A nursery full of babies should never be without a trained and licensed nurse."

So ten seconds after Demyan left my side, maybe three or four beats into the system-wide cacophony of enraged adults, every baby in the nursery erupted crying again, me included. I wasn't frightened by allegedly grown people yelling at each other. Not really. Mama was there and I knew no matter how angry she became, my grandmother would never let anything bad happen. Not to me. Instinctively, I'd caught on to my fellow babies' thinking and joined in the subterfuge. The adults might calm down if we gave them something louder to worry about.

* * *

43

Infants United. Our ruse worked stupidly well. Nurses Betty and Kayla interrupted their smoking-versus-bathroom dialogue to attend us, the loudest first, of course, and Mama halted her attack on Demyan to navigate the baby tank's center aisle and wrap me in her soft, loving arms. Her warm, comforting happiness enveloped me. Mama was an electric blanket set neither on low nor high, but perfect.

"You're coming home, little babe," Mama said. "It was decided before we came to see about the ruckus."

I didn't believe her—not at first. The news sounded too good. Guess I was super stunned. What drove the message home only seconds later, however, was seeing Emily and Demyan in the hallway, my mother no doubt giving her pink-haired friend the bad news about my homecoming. Big Pink made that ugly face again. And we all heard her groan.

Was that smoke that puffed from her nose?

Mama rocked me in her arms and studied me. "I told Emily what was in my heart—that I'd never live another happy day if we signed you over for adoption. You belong to us. You're our flesh and blood. Our Noelle. I told her if she's too busy to raise you, I will."

I believed her this time, and my heart shinnied up my throat. Every expectation had changed so fast, my reasoning seemed to slow. Mama was taking me home. Mama loved and wanted me, even if Emily didn't, or wasn't sure yet.

Though other babies in the maternity ward had no one, and I had Mama, my gut still ached. When Emily left with Demyan, the two of them had hustled through the maternity ward EXIT doors like kids running from the last day of school. For me, that image shrunk the world into one single fact. My own mother wanted nothing to do with me.

Maybe Emily was too young to understand the normal course of nature. For a fact, I knew she hadn't gotten down with nature past the sex part, or where boy meets girl and they fell in love. She needed to study the birds and the bees and the bunnies beyond animal mating rituals and procreative habits. I couldn't believe some of the books she'd read. Apparently, her education lacked the specific knowledge that when love produced a family, parents took care of their children. Think mother bears, Emily. Right? Birds hatching their eggs in a nest and bringing food.

Thinking about Emily and Demyan, wondering where they were off to, I knew Big Pink would be no help advancing my theories on family. Six people, including two teachers, had told Emily to watch out for, or stay away from, Demyan Kinsky. Demyan was an unsuitable friend, one said, a troublemaker and "the kind of girl who'll get you in trouble." The last old-fashioned prediction, from a widowed algebra teacher, Mrs. Macon, had been particularly prophetic. Yes, Demyan had introduced Emily to Billy Wallace. The boy who got her pregnant. So there was that. But apparently the term troublemaker was hardly a warning to Emily and most of her friends. From what I knew about them, I'd say TROUBLE in all caps was the very reason Emily *wanted* to hang with Demyan.

Nobody else Emily knew had tattoos, a ring in their nose or pink hair.

How exciting.

Demyan hadn't been nice to Emily at first, but after Demyan's two-week suspension from school, most of her friends had ditched her. Emily was a bit confused by the term oral sex—what the boy expected *exactly*—but Demyan had been caught in the boy's restroom doing whatever it was, exactly. A week after returning to school, Emily had seen Demyan wandering the cafeteria with a lunch tray but not finding a welcome.

Emily had waved at her.

Demyan scrambled along the hospital corridor, Emily trying to keep up. Demyan was anxious and getting salty for some fresh air and a smoke. Maybe a hit or two off the joint in her purse if nobody with a badge was around. She should move to Colorado. Tears rimmed her eyes and her throat squeaked while breathing. Felt like a noose around her neck, not a scarf. Emily deciding to keep the baby had produced physical reactions, and Demyan's own strong feelings were a surprise to her. Apparently losing her best friend was an emotional experience.

Demyan glanced at her. Best friend? Hell, these days Emily was practically her *one and only* friend. Thirteen-hundred kids in their high school, Emily Soria was one of only three or four human beings willing to eat lunch with her or say "hi" in the school hallways. Except for the teachers, only Emily noticed if Demyan attended classes or not. And now Emily would be spending every dusty minute of every dusty day with her baby.

Billy's baby.

Demyan removed a cigarette from her purse, slipped the filter between her teeth and fired her plastic lighter. "I can't believe you let your mother talk you into taking that kid home."

"Can I have one of those?" Emily said.

"I only have four left. And your mother's going to be out any second...with that kid. Why would you name it Noelle?"

"It's Christmas. Why not? I didn't know what to do. I haven't thought about baby names."

Demyan sucked on her menthol cigarette, thought better of her previous decision and offered her rare school chum one of the four remaining filter tips. How embarrassing would eating alone be, all those teachers and cafeteria workers watching her eat by herself. She might have to forget lunch, and a state-supported meal was the only one her mom would pay for.

"Thanks," Emily said. "Can I borrow your lighter?"

Demyan smiled. "Sure. Did your mother say she'd help you with the baby, or are you going to drop out of school?"

Emily lowered her eyes to blow the smoke down. "I'm going to stay in school. If I quit, I have to get a job."

"Well, you have only one more semester anyway. Unless you're going to college. Are you sure it's Billy's baby?"

Emily made a face. "I'm not lying. He's the only guy I've ever had sex with, so yeah, I'm sure."

"You going to tell him?"

"I'm sure he already knows. Someone from school would have called. Didn't you tell him yet?"

"No, I wouldn't tell him. That's your business. But I don't know how to reach hm. I heard his father's not giving out the number in Los Angeles. Maybe you couldn't reach him anyway."

"Who told you that?"

"I don't remember, but you shouldn't wait forever to try. You need to let him know you've had his baby. You don't want him to hear it from someone else."

Emily shrugged.

The hospital entrance buzzed open. Mrs. Soria strolled outside holding the baby in her arms, the kid wrapped up and bundled for an assault on Mt. Everest. Emily and her baby were so lucky. Demyan had never known either of her grandmothers, or ever experienced that kind of protective love. For a decade, the Kinsky family had consisted of Demyan and her mother, an unhappy forty-five-year-old widow who'd lost her husband in Afghanistan and worked alongside her daughter in a bagel and sandwich joint.

Demyan had to worry about herself. No one else would. She didn't have doting parents, a house and a family, a mother who bought her children stuff, who washed her clothes and made her meals. Demyan owned two pairs of jeans, four pair of underwear and a handful of blouses and athletic tops. She had to wash clothes for school practically every day. She understood life was a horror show unless you had money, and there weren't many ways to get rich. At eighteen, she figured the easiest way was marriage. And Billy Wallace would be perfect. He sang and played guitar in his own band. He was *the* stud of the school. Plus, the Wallaces had money. His father owned the local Chevrolet agency. Billy always had cash because he worked at his dad's car dealership after school and every summer. He'd done all kinds of different things, learning about cars. A mechanic's assistant. Sales in the showroom. Accounting. Even chassis and body repair in the underground body shop.

Billy would run the business someday. Billy Wallace would be rich.

A familiar car pulled up at the curb near the hospital's main entrance. Demyan recognized Mr. Soria's half-century-old relic. Who wouldn't? Demyan retreated deeper into the bamboo landscaping behind the smoker's bench and tugged on Emily's arm to come with her. They didn't have much more time together. What a nutty old hag Emily's mother was, making Emily keep the baby. Stupid, really. Mrs. Soria thought Emily was old enough to raise a kid but not to smoke?

Twenty yards away, Mr. Soria jogged behind his car toward his wife and the baby. One thing about that old car of his, the engine was smooth, so smooth Demyan couldn't tell if it was running or not. Mr. Soria opened the door for them, but Mrs. Soria hesitated, checking for her daughter. She couldn't see them behind the clumps of thick bamboo.

Demyan stared at her friend. "I can't believe you're really going to do this."

"I have to," Emily said. "And I have to go, too."

Demyan shook her head. Emily wasn't smart about boys, maybe life. Truly, she didn't know anything about anything except maybe singing and drawing little hearts with initials in them. Emily had sex without using birth control, let that drunken Billy hop on without a condom, a guy who didn't even like her. He'd slept with everybody in the senior class. Emily couldn't take care of a baby. She was a baby herself.

"You can't let your mother rule you forever," Demyan said.

"I know."

Emily crushed out her half-smoked cigarette. She left Demyan in the bamboo and a cloud of menthol cigarette smoke. Demyan glanced in the over-flowing ashtray, one of those black cylinders with a tiny hole near the top. From inside the tube, Emily's crushed cigarette still smoked. Fifty cents, gonzo. A spoiled brat, Emily was. No clue that times were tough, or how scarce decent jobs had become, how hard money was to earn.

Demyan tugged her coat tighter as the Sorias drove away. She lit a joint and remembered something in that brochure the child services lady had offered everyone. There'd been a toll-free phone number printed inside, an anonymous hot line where people could call the state to report parents or guardians who might be abusing children.

She sucked deeply on the marijuana. If Emily wouldn't stand up to her mother, maybe Demyan could stand up for her. Salty thing to do, for sure. What she had in mind. What she could report. But maybe Emily would thank her someday.

Should she really do it? Was she that mean?

When Demyan finished the joint, she flipped the remains into the bamboo jungle and headed back inside the hospital to find one of those brochures.

SEVEN

Santa Clauses, reindeer, nutcrackers, snowmen and angels still decorated Mama's house, as did her three, fully loaded Christmas trees, so when we came home from the hospital that night I finally saw Mama's famous spread with my own eyes. Wow. The house was dressed for the holiday party, Mama and Papi's annual celebration of family and love, and in those first moments back, Mama holding me, all those happy trimmings and finery, I knew my heart would always cherish and look forward to Christmas. The sights and sounds and the feelings would define happiness for the rest of my life.

Mama whispered to me that one room in the house was being changed. I couldn't imagine what she was talking about, and wondered the whole time as she carried me down the long hall. Everything smelled clean and washed. Thuds and squeaks greeted us from the far end of a narrow carpeted hall. Inside what Mama had previously called her sewing alcove—an enlarged hall closet— Phillip assembled some kind of giant wooden cage with a screwdriver. What kind of animal would they keep inside that thing?

"That's your new crib," Mama said.

What?

"Where you sleep at night."

Mama must have seen terror on my face.

"It's not as bad as it looks," she said.

The contraption grew on me, especially after Phillip finished assembling the soft-cornered, wooden pieces and the thick, cushioned mattress. Mama let me touch the polished wood. Smooth across my fingertips. The lack of bars and other restraints across the yawning top encouraged me as well. The overall size included much more space than the bassinette I'd existed in at the hospital, and although the crib qualified as a cage, I could easily crawl out anytime I wanted. No top to the crib. I was free to roam. Once I learned to crawl of course. My kicks had grown awesome, but I needed to expand my repertoire. The new crib looked like a place I could grow in.

I couldn't imagine where she'd found the time, but Mama had even decorated my new digs with a three-foot chest of drawers and a *Snow White* lamp on top. A blue and yellow, *Sponge Bob* bedspread would cover the mattress when Phillip finished. Pink flowered wallpaper covered the walls.

I choked up I was so happy, and I remember thinking I'd won my struggle for a loving home. That Emily was nowhere to be seen should have warned me.

I did whatever I could think of to make my surprise intrusion easier on Mama and Papi, and for the first few days everything seemed to go splendidly. Emily lived there, too, of course, but she had school in the day and went out almost every night with Demyan. Emily only bothered with me when Mama made her change my dirty pants and hug me.

The last few days, Emily might have warmed a tad. A touch. Maybe. But Mama and Papi acted like my mom and dad, and Mama ruled like a queen. Discipline and routine wore the crown. I went to bed every night at seven after a bath, even if I'd napped a lot and wasn't tired. Mama left me to play in my new crib, told me to make up stories with the stuffed animals she'd bought. My favorites were the giraffe and the hippopotamus, the names such wonderful, amazing words.

I felt safe with Mama and Papi, even alone in my crib. One or both of them always watched TV or read a book downstairs, or was sleeping close by in their bedroom twenty feet down the hall. The only time I bothered them was the first night. I woke up from a dream and couldn't remember where I was at first. I cut loose two frightened screams before remembering why *Snow White* stared at me from the top of a small dresser. Both Mama and Papi came running to my rescue and neither was angry, although Papi didn't stare into my eyes and smile the same way Mama did—as if I were the most precious thing on earth.

So we had several days of bliss, and then, the way Mama liked to describe events—Mama often mixing her metaphors—something rotten hit the fan in Denmark.

Our troubles began with the doorbell. Mama held me in her arms when she answered, so together we discovered the lady from child services on our doorstep, the same Barbara Foster we'd met at the hospital. Red tangled hair. White freckled skin and glasses. She smelled of freshly printed newspaper.

Foster gazed at me superficially, acknowledging my presence but not my importance. With a title like child services officer, you'd think she'd be more interested in me, the actual newborn. Instead, Foster studied the notepaper and documents attached to her clipboard.

"May I come in?" she said.

I didn't like her voice. She'd sounded nervous. At least low on confidence. I suspected that meant some kind of bad news was forthcoming. I had a hunch what it might be, too.

"Why?" Mama said.

"There's been a complaint...possible child abuse."

"What? Who complained?"

"That's not important."

"It is to me," Mama said.

"I'm sorry," Foster said. "Our sources are promised anonymity if they request it. But I need to come inside, Ms. Soria. That's the law."

Mama hesitated. "So because some anonymous person complains, you get to barge into my home and snoop around?" Foster adjusted her glasses. "No, I get to come into your home and snoop around because your daughter previously abandoned her child in the hospital and admitted to a complete absence of prenatal care. These circumstances require child services to investigate any and all complaints."

Mama still wasn't going to let her inside, her body language growing even more defensive. My grandmother's shoulders and hips ballooned in the doorway like a wild animal puffing up before battle.

"All I need to do—and I'll do it quickly—is walk through the house," Foster said, "make sure there are no obvious danger zones for the child. Things like visible firearms, sharp objects, unsafe electrical outlets. I also need to ask some questions, but not many."

Remaining in full-protection mode, Mama assumed the demeanor of a polite rhinoceros. "This is not a convenient time."

Foster sighed. "I can easily come back with two state troopers, Mrs. Soria. Their cars will be parked outside your home with the lights flashing, and they will be armed while they escort me throughout the property and inside every room of your house. But let's you and I do that now—skip all that trooper stuff. What do you say?"

The way she'd spoken and the words themselves sounded rehearsed. Too informal, like phrases they taught you to use on unpleasant mothers and fathers blocking admission. But the threat of armed law enforcement stomping through her home sure worked on my grandmother. One of the neighbors had lost their home to foreclosure earlier that year, and the sheriff's deputies had put the father in handcuffs when he resisted eviction. The street still gossiped about it. Mama deflated her posture and ushered Foster inside.

First thing Foster did was take pictures. She held up a new iPhone and snapped four quick shots of the living room, each in a different direction.

Mama frowned. "What are you doing?"

"I need photographs for my file," Foster said. "It's standard procedure."

She used her thumbs to type, emailing her new photos of the Soria living room with a short text message to someone, and Mama and I leaned in to see. There were two addresses on her screen, one, our local child services office, and two, the department's statewide headquarters. Three people had been listed as recipients, her county supervisor and two managers in the main investigations office.

Mama growled before she could speak. "I want you to stop. Right now. This is a terrible invasion of our privacy."

Foster shook her head while she strode into the den. "I am doing what's required by my agency and by the law, Mrs. Soria, and I wouldn't object if I were you. The condition and cleanliness of your home can only help your case. The cheerfulness of all these Christmas decorations says nice things, too. Most of the homes I see are—"

"What case?"

Foster photographed the den. "Any complaint generates a case number."

Mama growled.

We followed Foster into the kitchen where again she took four photographs.

"So there's the baby, the mother, grandma and grandpa living in the house, is that right?" Foster said.

"There's also Phillip," Mama said. "Emily's brother."

"So there's an uncle living here as well?"

"Yes. Phillip. He's fifteen."

"Can I meet him?"

"He's in school with Emily. They'll be home this afternoon."

Foster nodded. "Okay, good to know. I'll make their testing appointments for the early evening. Is tomorrow okay?"

"What are you talking about? What tests? What appointments?"

"Everyone who lives in the house will have to be drug tested. That's the procedure in these types of cases."

"Drug tested? Why?"

"That's the nature of the complaint...that several members of the newborn's household are drug addicts. That is, obviously, not in the best interests of the child."

If Mama had transformed into a polite rhinoceros on her doorstep, she now became a raging elephant ready to trash whatever and whomever got in her way. Her chest puffed out, her jaw clanked shut, and she advanced inexorably toward Foster like an earthmover clearing brush. I couldn't see the look in Mama's eyes, but Foster sure didn't like it.

"Please calm down, Mrs. Soria."

Foster back-peddled with great skill, but telling agitated women of Italian descent to *calm down* was a no-no. In fact, I'd be willing to bet that phrase has caused anger in Italian women as long as there have been women from Italy. Maybe women in general. I don't just *believe* this. I *know* it in my genes. Veins and arteries bulged along both sides of Mama's neck, and Foster found no way to resist. Before the child services lady could summon enough courage to stand firm, all three of us had traveled back to the front doorway.

"You get out of my house this instant," Mama said. "You have no authority to test my blood—or my patience."

"I most certainly do," the lady said. "And a family court judge is waiting to potentially sign a warrant for your arrest if you will not comply."

Foster may have had the law on her side, but that didn't tip the scales of justice in the Soria household. In Mama's house, only Mama wore justice's blindfold.

She raised a hand onto Foster's shoulder and stepped forward, shoving Foster outside the house. Mama slammed the door.

***

In Emily's bedroom that night, me in the bassinette watching, Emily doodled with her felt-tip pen. Working at the roll-top oak desk Papi had purchased after she'd announced her desire to write world-famous poetry, Emily touched the marker two-thirds of the way up a sheet of white typing paper. First making a quick V, she extended the right wing of the V up and out, drawing a circling bulge that fell at an angle to a spot at the bottom of her initial V. By next creating a mirror image of that first line, Emily produced a perfect cartoon heart. Red marker on stark white paper. I knew what went inside her big blood-red organ, too—a B and a W. Billy Wallace's initials. She'd drawn so many of those hearts the last few months, I half-worried she might be going batty.

Another explanation would be that the hearts, at least in Emily's subconscious, involved sex. But Emily hadn't been a big reader of psychological books, and I felt unqualified to suggest such a diagnosis. More likely, Emily thought drawing little hearts with BW inside equaled positive thinking. If you wished for something every day, and you really wanted it, the positive vibrations of your brain could make stuff happen. That's what Demyan had told her, what the book Demyan showed her had claimed. Among other odd assertions. What Emily believed, making hearts and meditating about Billy couldn't do any harm. So if she enjoyed drawing for a little while every day, why not make hearts?

I worried about her though. For one thing, Emily no longer understood what she wanted out of life. For the longest time she'd wanted to be a teacher, or maybe a nurse. Something where she could help people. Then she'd wanted to write, help society in a big way by writing inspirational books. But that morphed sometimes into drawing and painting, and the last nine months, she'd dreamed of singing professionally.

On the night I'd been conceived, music had generated as much excitement in Emily as Billy. The sound and the crowd had merged so well, the room and the players—Emily the back-up singer included—had become melody and song itself, a feeling of ecstasy near drug-rush strength.

I worried also because Emily's self-confidence had taken a hit. Not recognizing she'd been pregnant had been a giant face-slap. My birth had made her feel less than intelligent. That nice nurse Betty had tried to help. She'd told Emily because she'd hidden the pregnancy so well, Emily's personality must include a strong and vibrant will. Emily mirrored the type of rare spirit that could accomplish virtually anything.

Emily thought Betty was nice to say that, the information well-intentioned, but I knew Emily denied *any* positive side effects of my cryptic birth, even me. Although honestly, some feelings were hard for me to decipher. About Billy, my mother behaved in ways I didn't understand, exhibiting feelings and conflicts I hadn't learned about from her books and movies. She had hidden things from me, and herself maybe, secrets from the time before I was around—one big secret from the very night I'd been conceived.

I watched Emily finish her red heart and reach for a new sheet of white paper. I yawned and went over again every detail Emily remembered about the night she and Billy had created me. Maybe I'd overlooked something the last twelve times. Emily had spoken to her brother Phillip last night about singing in Billy's band, how her one-night gig happened. Phillip had been curious ever since super-jock Billy Wallace had dropped out of school.

What Emily had told Phillip, recreating the scene for him, Demyan had called after school, asked if Emily could get out of the house that night. If Emily could lace up and cut loose, Demyan told her to wear black jeans and a flashy top and to meet at the Lucky Lady Club on Washington Boulevard.

"I don't have fake ID," Emily said.

"You don't need ID. Billy's going to let us in."

"Billy Wallace?"

"Who do you think?"

"But Billy isn't twenty-one either."

"He's got a gig there tonight. His band is playing. He told me he'd send someone at ten o'clock to let us in the back door."

"How cool that Billy asked you to come hear the band," Emily said.

"Hear nothing. You and I are the back-up singers."

"What?"

"You heard me. He wants chick back-up singers for the second set."

"How are we going to do that? We've never rehearsed. Do you even know the songs?"

"The second set is old Motown stuff you've heard a thousand times. Your father plays the stuff on the radio. Billy's band turned up the songs, going half rap, but you'll know where the back-up vocal parts are. You'll just hear them. Watch me. I'll sing thirds, you do fifths like we always do it."

Emily's memories of having sex with Billy were vague, more focused on the emotional aspects than the technical, so I was sure she'd hidden things from me. Emily could do that with events and people she disliked, bad things that happened. By nature, Emily blocked them out of her memory.

Though Emily had goofed around singing with Demyan many an afternoon and evening, Emily had never sung with a professional band. She had no idea how powerful the drums and amplified guitars would feel when played together so well, how much passion a tight group of musicians could push from her body and vocals. It was like being an instrument yourself and having the music play *you*. During the last number, a rap version of an old '60s hit, *Heat Wave*, Emily lost herself inside the beat, those people all dancing in time, that feeling you weren't playing the music anymore, you *were* music. Afterward, talking to Billy in the dark, he said she'd been lucky, that the feeling of 'music playing you' didn't happen every time. But wasn't it wonderful?

There was the sex, yes, but then something else happened that night, something equally life changing for Emily. But what?

I have a hunch, but Emily had blocked too much of the memory, too many of the individual images for me to be certain. Worse, she'd barred from her consciousness ninety percent of the episode's emotional content. Whatever moved her so much, I knew only the experience had been frightening.

After they'd made love in the band's break room, Billy had taken out a rectangular, tan leather shaving kit from his larger carry-all, a suitcase-size sports bag he always brought on gigs to hold his personal microphones, extra strings for his guitar and picks, a tuner, plus whatever booze, candy bars and other junk he wanted for the night.

The smaller, tan-leather container had a zipper on top and reminded Emily of an old travel shaving kit Papi's father used keep in her bathroom when he'd visited. Inside, Emily's grandfather had stored his razor, comb, toothbrush and half a dozen pill bottles.

But what had been inside Billy's?

Back in the present, Emily drew her seventh cartoon heart in five minutes. Each had BW written inside. My mother sure had focus, and I could picture every tiny feature of that leather travel kit my great grandfather used to carry with him. But whatever had been *inside* Billy's leather case had totally freaked Emily out. She didn't want to *think* about the contents again, nor remember any of what had happened over the following two hours.

I had a hunch but hoped I was wrong.

EIGHT

Weeks passed. Another savage snow storm had quieted, and Mama's opposition to Barbara Foster's requests had vanished along with her Christmas decorations by the time Emily and I returned from our latest court-ordered drug test. In the dining room where we'd all eaten that special holiday dinner, two plain white candles burned in cold pewter candlesticks. Even the smell of Mama's Christmas trees was gone. I especially missed the dolls and holiday knick-knacks previously adorning the mantle, bookshelves and sideboard.

Emily carried me in the dark blue bassinette with a zip-out liner and a perforated mattress. The bassinette was part of a convertible stroller, and with all the blankets and stuffed toys inside with me, I was crammed in like a sausage. Emily left me in the bassinette so she wouldn't have to hold me, positioning me on the dining room table near the kitchen. I imagined myself as a giant roasted pig, apple-mouthed for the next holiday feast.

Outside, snowflakes floated across the yard in a slow, left-to-right drift, the morning's storm having slowed to gentler patterns. Barren oak tree branches collected top-half covers of white fluff. We couldn't hear a sound, outside or in. Mama and Papi's house sat empty and silent, Papi at work fixing Chevrolets and Mama maybe shopping. The forced-air heater kicked on with a thud seconds later, interrupting the hush, but by the time the climate control system reacted and hot air blew from the vents near Mama's spotless floor, a deep stillness had returned.

"Looks like we're all alone," Emily said.

I smiled at her. That had been the first complete sentence Emily ever spoke to me. The whole time in the hospital, at home and even at this morning's visit to the medical testing facility where we waited and waited, Emily had kept me beside her in the bassinette but never talked. Maybe a *goo-goo* here and there. I hadn't cried when the nurse stuck me with a needle and drained blood. The nurse had commented to Emily how brave I was, how resilient. Emily smiled at the nurse but she didn't even look at me.

Thrilled now by her speech, the personal nature of her words, 'Looks like we're all alone,' I offered Emily a joyful squeal. Naturally, my mother turned her head exactly at that moment and didn't see. Emily instead gazed at herself in the sofa-sized mirror hanging over Mama's antique sideboard. The reflection made her appear unwell, with pale skin and sunken eyes—worse than the fatigue you'd expect after delivering a baby. She appeared exhausted, maybe running the fever suggested by her bright pink cheeks and the sweat beneath her eyes.

Emily had changed in the last few weeks. All of us in the family had noticed. She'd wanted nothing to do with home, family and babies, any kind of life like her parents. She wanted to travel, meet new people and see new places every day. Sounded good not being tied down to one town, one job and one guy forever. More babies to raise on lousy salaries. The financial struggle. But lately something had changed. As if a new organ had been created inside her, an organ that issued commands and sucked energy from her ambitions, she'd stopped talking about music and art so much. Instead, she dreamt of her and Billy on a beach, once with a small child between them, holding hands. Must be some kind of natural chemical inside her, she'd told Phillip, trying to make a mother out of the rock star Emily had imagined she wanted to be.

The doorbell chimed, shattering our quiet, and Emily left me perched on the dining table while she went to answer. I figured it was a package delivery, Mama buying all kinds of baby stuff online this week, but when Emily opened the door and that familiar voice said "Hi," once again I recalled that roasted pig. I hoped Demyan wasn't carrying an apple.

I believed instinctively that Emily's friend Big Pink had materialized there to harm us. I heard evil in her speech—a low-pitched hum of raw deceit. What was the feature she possessed that made Emily befriend her? Obviously something about Demyan had struck my mother blind. Maybe it was the pink spiked hair. Or the steel knob through her tongue to pleasure boys, girls and bisexuals throughout the western world. Oh no wait, I just figured everything out. Demyan had on the same tan shorts and black halter top she wore yesterday. Emily loved to be around her because Demyan often issued a faint aroma of body odor.

"I brought a present for the baby," Demyan said.

Probably a carton of rat poison.

"You're kidding?" Emily said.

"Of course I'm kidding. Duh!" She rolled her eyes to make sure we understood. "Where's your mother?"

"I don't know. We only this minute got home from our drug test."

"Your mother's not here? Fantastic. Let's drop off the kid. You know you want to. You told me so before. There's a Catholic church eight blocks away that accepts newborns, no questions asked. I called."

"My mother would kill me," Emily said. "She might kill you, too."

Demyan's *suggestion* almost killed me. My heart couldn't decide to jump, skip, dance or boogie on down. Gee, Demyan, thanks for coming over to throw me away.

Demyan stretched her hand out for the bassinette. "The hell

with your mother. She's not around. Come on. Do you want to spend the rest of your life changing paper pants filled with crap?"

A creepy electric charge straightened the fuzz on my head as Demyan yanked me off the table, the bassinette swinging wildly side to side. A white cloth belt cinched my waist, but the fit was loose and the belt too thin. I doubted I'd remain contained much longer if Demyan kept handling me like a bag of onions. As she lugged me toward the door, a noise stopped her.

"Yellow," Mama said.

Mama always announced herself that way, my grandmother being her goofy self with the transformation of *hello*. Whoever heard her was supposed to answer *yellow* back so she'd know if anyone else was home. Instead, Emily used the distraction to snatch me away from Demyan.

I gasped for air. I hadn't realized I'd been holding my breath. Mama stayed in the kitchen.

Emily frowned at her friend and whispered, "I think you should leave, Demyan. That was a really scary thing you just did. Weird. And it makes me think you're the one who called child services and told them my family smoked pot. Are you?"

"No."

Emily didn't look fooled. Of course it was Demyan. Who else but Big Pink even knew a child lived here?

"You're acting this way because the baby is Billy's, aren't you?" Emily said. "You're jealous he and I hooked up, that he might have feelings for me."

Demyan sniffed. "To Billy, you were nothing but a piece. A booty call."

In the kitchen, Mama unloaded two old-fashioned, brown paper grocery bags, pretending she couldn't hear. But when Demyan grunted and hurried into the kitchen, anxious to leave through the back, Mama blocked her exit. No whiff of Christmas tree resin lingered, so for my grandmother, the season of goodwill had expired.

"Did you call my daughter a piece?" Mama said.

Demyan smirked. "Yeah. And a lousy one, too, according to Billy."

Mama tried to squeeze Big Pink against the granite countertop, twisting to shift her own bulk. But Demyan was too quick and squeezed through. She jumped out the kitchen door.

Hightailing it, Papi would have said.

If I thought too much about Demyan and her actions, I had to worry, not only about myself and Emily, but about mankind in general. Nature obviously created the family unit for a specific and important function. Parents were needed to protect children while they grew up. Survival of the species. People who wanted to destroy that—people like Demyan—were antisocial at best. I tried to banish Big Pink and her hate from my thoughts.

Late the next morning, while Mama fed me vitamin-infused baby formula and Papi made a brunch of peanut butter on toast, we heard back from the state's child services department. A phone call arrived with those drug-test results. Mama accepted the information since Phillip and Emily were minors and both at school, but Papi and I could read the headlines on Mama's pinched forehead.

"Are you sure?" she said.

She listened for another minute, said "Yes, I understand," then slapped the kitchen house phone back on its wall mount. The collision of plastic on plastic rattled sharply.

Mama stared at her husband. "Emily and Phillip both tested positive for marijuana."

Papi showed no surprise.

"They found marijuana in your blood, too," Mama said.

"What? This is truly hard to believe. I took two or three hits off a joint with Rafael and Tony last Saturday. That is true. I went over to help Rafael put new brakes on his El Camino, remember?

We had the radio on in the garage, laughing, like when we were in high school. But it was only one joint...and I only had a couple of puffs, I swear. How could they—"

"It doesn't matter," Mama said. "You tested positive. The lady said the stuff lasts for months in your fat cells."

"But it was nothing."

"It's not *nothing*." Mama's dark eyes turned black. "Four of the five people living in my house tested positive for drugs. The baby had traces of pot, too. There's a chance we could lose Noelle."

Papi blinked. "For pot? How could this be?"

"Exactly what I said. But Noelle had no prenatal care. Her teenage mother left the hospital without her, a specific act constituting abandonment. And the mother, baby and two others living in the house—including one of two adults—tested positive for illegal substances. Drugs. There's already a long list of judges who'll sign a court order saying Noelle is at risk."

Papi swallowed a piece of toast. "Do we have to tell the children?"

"Tell them they both failed the drug test? Of course. I'm going to kick their butt, too."

"No, I mean tell them *I* failed."

"Of course. You'll have to go to rehabilitation classes together, plus at least three Narcotics Anonymous meetings a week."

"What? No way I am doing that," Papi said.

Mama pressed her right forefinger against Papi's chest. "Oh yes you will. And you'll do it with a smile on your face, too, Senor Ernesto Soria, because if every single person in this family doesn't test clean next week, the week after and every week until this cloud is lifted, child services will file court papers to remove Noelle from our home."

Mama glanced at me in my bassinette, trying to smile, but my grandmother's eyes glistened with tears. Papi wouldn't look at me. He stared at the drifting snow outside the kitchen window.

* * *

I knew we headed in the direction of a substance-abuse counseling session, Papi's first, but the venue surprised me. A school auditorium? Papi drove Mama's car because he said his '61 Impala hardtop was a target for vandals, especially in a strange parking lot, especially at night, especially at the county's biggest high school.

The older people looked like Papi, working class men and women, everybody in waterproof vest jackets or full snow gear, half of them accompanied by teenage children wearing blue jeans and sweat shirts. Hoods up. Emily carried me in my bassinette, the only newborn. There weren't that many smiles, but I gave one back to every friendly face who bent over me. No one seemed happy to be there.

Fifteen or twenty people waited inside the cone-shaped, 400-seat auditorium, most of them seated in the second and third row of cramped folding chairs. Papi tried to lead us to the empty first tier, but Emily chose the second, and Phillip kept walking, moving someplace I couldn't see. Another two dozen people of all ages followed us inside over the next five minutes, and at the top of the hour, a female police officer in a pale blue uniform walked onto the elevated stage. She sighed behind the podium and pressed a button. A movie screen lit up behind her, the back-lighted monitor stretching three-quarters of the way across the stage.

"I call your attention to this list," the officer said. "If more than one of these symptoms apply to you, the odds are good— no, the odds are excellent you're an alcoholic or a drug abuser. Since you are here tonight because a judge, state investigator or court appointed mediator has ordered you to, the first of those symptoms—problems—is already on your scorecard. I see puzzled faces, but I assure you ladies and gentleman, forcing you from your home at night is in fact a family problem."

A young man, an assistant, walked among the rows at audience level. He stopped to hand Emily a stack of papers. "Please take one and pass down the rest."

I managed a glance before Emily stuck the wadded flyer in her pocket. The words printed on the paper matched those on the movie screen.

Has your drug or alcohol use caused a problem with work, school or family?

Have you experienced changes in your appetite or sleep patterns?

Any sudden weight loss—or weight gain?

A deterioration in physical appearance, personal grooming habits?

Any drop in performance at work or school?

A sudden change in friends, favorite hangouts and hobbies?

Are you subject to sudden mood swings, irritability or angry outbursts?

Have you lied about your substance abuse?

The police officer was pleasant and entertaining, going over her personal battle with substance addiction and how a meeting like the one we currently attended had launched her on a path to recovery. A practiced speaker, the attractive brunette dazzled us with bright blue eyes, a strong voice, a compelling smile and obvious truths about our lives.

"Beer, cocaine, marijuana, ecstasy, Xanax or heroin—the addiction itself is all the same," she said. "One is too many and a thousand is never enough."

On the way home, Papi kept quiet. He usually had a funny story to tell about the dealership's other auto mechanics, often a prank engineered during the work day. But not that night. He waited until we'd pulled into our driveway twenty minutes later to explain.

"Wait a minute before you two get out," Papi said. "I need to say something. No, I need to apologize. But I do not know where or how to begin."

"You don't need to be sorry for anything," Emily said. "You've been a great father."

"No," Papi said. "No, I have not."

"Start at the beginning," Phillip said.

Phillip sat beside his father. Emily and I occupied the back bench seat, me in my trusty bassinette. Papi turned off the engine, pitching us all into darkness. The engine began to cool, making pops and clicks while he gathered his thoughts. The air smelled of the lemon oil Papi used to clean the dashboard.

"When I saw those questions on the stage tonight, 'Are there problems at work or home, have your friends changed?' I began to read them thinking, I hope I do not discover that my children are drug addicts. But three or four questions in, I realized I was the substance abuser. I smoke way too much marijuana. I drink too much. I have been irritable, shouting at Phillip's basketball referees. I have gained weight, and your mother says I have let other aspects of my appearance decline. And I have lied about smoking, especially to your mother. Clearly, I am the addict, not my children."

Phillip shrugged. "Lots of people your age smoke pot. It's no big deal."

"I believe it may be a big deal, Philip. I did not previously understand what that lady officer made clear. Some people can drink, smoke or even snort once in a while. They can take it or leave it because they are not addicts. I cannot. I would keep smoking more and more because that is what I have done now for several years. And I would do this even though the state would take Noelle."

"So quit for a while," Emily said. "You'll be fine. If I can do it, you can, too."

"Yes, we must all quit now, even if we are not addicts. All of us."

Phillip sighed. "But why apologize, Papi? If we quit, everything will be all right."

"I must apologize for failing you. My father gave me excellent parenting advice two decades ago, and because he was a wonderful, loving father, I should have listened harder to what he told me. It was a lesson pertaining to this very problem."

Emily reached for me in my bassinette. She touched my cheek. "What did he say?"

"My father told me children do not do what you tell them to do. They do what you *do*."

NINE

Whiteout. After several days of steady snowfall, Mama and Papi's neighborhood resembled a winter apocalypse. The residential street between older, wood-frame houses had been plowed into a slippery white tunnel, the sides consisting of parked cars buried under mountains of ice and snow. Not a bad toboggan run. Thick tree branches dipped onto bleached lawns or, having already snapped, extended their broken wounds toward a gun-gray sky.

Papi kept his own sidewalks and driveway clear with snow salt and a shovel-like attachment for the twenty-year-old John Deer riding lawn mower he'd bought used at a yard sale. No doubt the city's plow operators hadn't been thrilled with Papi's little piles—mounds of snow collected from his own driveway and nudged into the municipal street—but neither had they complained or pushed Papi's snow back onto his property. When Mama carried me outside onto the front porch, the house appeared free of snow and ice from back door to driveway. The frigid air nipped my tender cheeks, but the stuff also tasted like pine-covered mountains. Refreshing.

"Hurry up," Mama said. "We're going to be late as it is."

Behind Mama and me, Emily grunted. "Like I'm supposed to care?"

Mama and I waited on the back porch, me in my bassinette,

Emily still inside the house. My seventeen-year-old mother had gone out the previous night and only returned twenty-five minutes ago, her clothes and appearance disheveled, her manner grumpy. As a result, the family would be late for our conflict resolution meeting with child services. Mama had to be there, too, even though she'd passed all the drug tests. Her tossing Barbara Foster from the house hadn't exactly worked in our favor, but the cops had never showed up, and Mama had agreed to the testing. Barbara Foster and the state seemed to be taking a wait-and-see attitude, choosing meeting over confrontation.

"You'd better start caring," Mama said. "Or you will regret that attitude for the rest of your life."

Emily showed in the doorway. "You're speaking in clichés again, Mama."

"They're clichés because they're true."

"Really? Because that sounds like when you say, do it because I'm your mama and I'm telling you to."

Emily finally trickled outside, and Mama reached quickly behind her to key the door. "Well, you should listen to your mother."

"See."

From the driveway, Papi lowered the car window. "Come on you two. We're late." He and Phillip sat inside Papi's antique Chevrolet, the souped-up engine running creamy, both of them grinning. What was it about tardiness in a woman that made men feel superior? As if they were never late, or ran around the house yelling, 'Where're my keys?'

Papi had owned two hot rod Chevys until last year when the house needed a new roof, and his black beauty, a '55 Chevy Bel Air, had to be sold. Papi said he wouldn't give up his '61 Impala until we were all in the homeless shelter.

After a warmer night, freezing temperatures had returned. As we scrambled across the porch, where Papi had installed an outdoor thermometer, the air hovered right between thirty-two and thirty-three degrees Fahrenheit. For the first time since Mama had knitted that silly hat for my fuzzy head, I was glad for the cover, fresh pine air aside. Mama grabbed the rail with her free hand to begin our descent of the porch steps. I got a major whiff of her perfume—Mama's fancy stuff, the *Chanel No. 5*.

Emily scooted past us on the stairs and avoided the brick walkway by leaping directly from the last cement tread onto the frozen front lawn, narrowly missing Mama's favorite flower pot. Mama gasped. Nothing grew inside the bright blue and yellow container during winter, but Mama had painted and fired the ginger jar-shaped earthenware herself.

"Be careful," Mama said. "You almost—"

Good thing I'd already guessed what Emily had almost done because Mama never finished that sentence. She'd quit because both of her feet had shot out from underneath her. She'd tromped off the porch steps onto our brick walk at normal speed, and though the water molecules on the cement steps remained liquid, the water on the brick had frozen. Mama had walked onto invisible ice.

Her first thought was to protect me from harm, apparently. She held the bassinette up like a torch, maybe hoping I wouldn't be first to hit the ground or a cement edge. There was a long moment where I hung in the air weightless, my next direction indeterminable, a vertical bassinette-babe floating in the cold still air. What a strange view of the world I had, my new knit hat pointed at the brick walkway, my feet at the sky. I remember images of the locked front door, the gray cement porch stairs and Mama's coat-covered shoulder, all of them one-hundred percent upside down.

I was scared. I just didn't know it yet. Mama's slip and the fall had come so fast, and my own moment of total helplessness arrived so unexpectedly, the only thing gripping me was shock and surprise. Mama held on to the bassinette, even as she first crashed into the brick, so my impact was half of what it could have been. But after Mama's initial landing, which had been accompanied by the sound of something cracking, Mama's fingers turned me loose. We caromed on the ice in different directions. Wind rushed across my face. I did a rebound and a ricochet that hammered my newly functioning organs. The thin bassinette strap cut into my tummy. Breakfast threatened to return where I could see and smell it. But Mama's efforts prevented a much worse outcome for me, and that's probably what got Mama hurt. She must have landed in a particularly awkward position because of holding the bassinette the way she had.

Eventually the bassinette and I slid to a halt. My transport vehicle lay on its side ten or twelve inches from the brick's end and a four-inch drop to the first stone of walkway across the lawn. My miniature body was pinched inside by that annoying, gut-poking strip of thin cloth. Mama sat up by then, holding her injured forearm, a perplexed look in her eyes. Papi and Phillip hurried in our direction.

Emily hovered on the lawn, frozen herself, her mouth wide open.

But a second later she kneeled beside me. "You poor thing."

She unhooked the bassinette strap and hugged me to her chest, a first for my mother, at least without Mama's orders behind it. Another first was me believing my mother emotionally cared about me. My own heart soared with her closeness. We were as near to being one person as we had ever been, as together as when connected by the umbilical cord. And this connection was a choice she'd made, not the unlucky result of a one-night sexual encounter. Holding me in her arms, Emily peeked beneath by knit cap, but found no wounds, nothing at all worth comment.

"Oh Jenny, are you hurt?" Papi said.

Mama's first name was Vincenza, Jenny for short. Papi always called her Mama around the house, but I guess her name became Jenny when Papi felt worried or upset. Though sitting up, Mama remained quiet and motionless on the brick walk, her rear end flat on the bricks with both legs straight out. Her brown eyes were as big as walnuts.

Emily shifted her gaze to see what I looked at. "Mama, are you okay?"

"Sure." Mama waved off Papi's help. "We're going to be very late to that meeting with Foster," she said. "We need to call."

Her voice rattled me, Mama's tone carrying an odd, hollow flatness. I wondered how badly she'd been hurt.

"Is Mama's arm broken?" Phillip said. "It looks funny."

I'd noticed that bump in her forearm. And there was that crack I'd heard. Could have been Mama's bone breaking. And when Papi examined her, a flash of horror preceding his calm smile, I understood we were headed again for the hospital. Not our child services meeting.

Mama finally allowed Papi to lift her. "We need to hurry," she said.

Papi smiled. "Jenny, my wife, we are on our way to the hospital emergency room, not the courthouse annex. Your arm is broken. In addition, I believe you may be in shock."

"I am *not* in shock," she said.

Papi knew better than to argue. "Excellent. It is very good you are not in shock. But either way, you must get up now and walk slowly with me to the car."

Papi tucked his arm tight around her waist. Phillip walked on Mama's other side, his arm lifting and supporting her. The Soria men employed careful steps, Emily and me following, my mother's attitude much toned down from her previous demeanor.

Could my mother be worried about someone besides herself?

We all packed into Papi's 1961 Chevy Impala, a car much like the man himself. The two-door hardtop was old fashioned, for sure, but the antique was nifty, too, spruced up, well-maintained and one-hundred percent operational. The engine ran like churned butter, as well as any car Papi ever owned, better than most half-million-dollar Ferraris or Lotuses, at least according to Phillip. His school friends asked him all the time about the

Chevy and its fuel-injected 327-cubic-inch power plant, maybe the best-running V-8 ever built. Plus, Papi could tune anything with absolute perfection. Backing out the driveway that day, I couldn't even hear the engine. Maybe a cat purring.

The hospital emergency room had grown familiar. Windowless green walls. A cocktail of antiseptic and human odors. The whispers of suffering and pain. A lack of open seating. Who knew so many people hurt themselves every day. The only surprise—and it shouldn't have been—most of the current patients had slipped and fallen on the morning ice like Mama. At least six of the nine people waiting had broken limbs in need of mending. The hospital had called for more orthopedic specialists and doctors, but Mama seemed destined for a major wait.

At Papi's insistence, one of the emergency room nurses checked Mama eyes, and as a result of what she'd seen, tested Mama's pulse and blood pressure. The nurse grunted loudly when the numbers came up on her hand-held machine. Something wasn't normal. Within two minutes, Mama rolled out of the waiting area in a wheelchair, headed for treatment space.

Papi hesitated, waiting for the nurse to guide her away. "Your mother is in shock," he whispered. "But do not worry, our Jenny is very tough."

Papi jockeyed between the injured and the worried to catch up with Mama in the wheelchair. He advanced with difficulty, shifting his hips and elbows like a wide receiver for the Dallas Cowboys. Phillip followed Papi as best he could. The young man was extremely athletic. Emily shifted her grip on the bassinette to walk behind her brother.

Papi stopped and waited for Emily to catch up. "It would be best if you two waited back there."

"We want to be with Mama," Phillip said.

Emily nodded. "Definitely."

Papi stared at his children, particularly Emily. All three of their faces loomed directly above me and the bassinette. I felt like a tourist at Mount Rushmore. I could see serious family questions in Papi's expression, although his queries did not concern matters of Mama's health. Papi was dying to ask about Emily's pregnancy and my birth.

"Better if Mama knows you are watching your baby," Papi said. "And I will need to speak with the doctors privately."

Phillip's shoulders sagged, but he'd never questioned his father in my presence. The dutiful son checked the waiting room and pointed Emily toward a recently vacated plastic seat. I hoped Emily didn't sit in it because that meant she'd most likely place my bassinette on the dirty tile floor.

"My baby's fine," Emily said. "I can watch her wherever I am."

Papi shook his head. "You should not bring a newborn into the hospital. Noelle has a brand new immune system, and this building is nothing if not a giant collection box for disease. Do not worsen her exposure by following your mother."

Emily's jaw chewed imaginary gum. "Can I have the car keys? I want to put her in the stroller and go for a walk."

TEN

Our family physician suggested a specific orthopedic surgeon to set Mama's broken arm. But the recommended sawbones was already mending fractures elsewhere and couldn't get to our hospital for hours, so Papi decided to drive the rest of us home and come back by himself to wait. Emily, Phillip and I wanted to stay with Mama, but a three-hour delay before surgery did sound gruesome, especially in a crowded waiting room.

Hashtag #hotandstinky.

On our way home, I wondered what the house would be like without Mama running the family like a Marine general. Funny how we liked being told what to do, at least by Mama, and even worried when the director took necessary time off. At the same time, Emily had acted differently after the accident. I looked forward to spending time with her, understanding better what had changed.

"I wonder who that is?" Papi said.

He jerked to a stop less than halfway in our driveway—behind a gray Ford. The strange car occupied most of the cement slab fronting our tiny garage, and Papi was forced to park his antique Chevy so the two left-side wheels rode up onto the frozen lawn. I wondered if the gray Ford usurping our driveway belonged to Demyan Kinsky.

The day sure had been a loser so far.

Before Papi shut off his engine, the strange Ford popped open up like a cooked clam. A familiar female clambered out into the cold bright sunshine. She wasn't Demyan, although about as welcome, at least on my invitation list. We'd been paid a surprise visit by Barbara Foster, the woman from child services. Red tangled hair. White freckled skin and glasses. The accountant who added up all her possibilities. Mama had tossed her from the house weeks ago, and prior to that, bargained with Foster in the hospital as prelude to my escape.

"We need to talk," Foster said.

My stomach turned sour.

Foster pulled a stack of documents from a leather purse the size of a briefcase. The group had collected on the thawing lawn beside her Ford and I figured a quick discussion loomed about why we'd missed the morning meeting. The lawn had grown brown patches of dormant grass while we'd been gone. Snow melted and dripped noisily from the roof. Papi had grumbled yesterday he needed to clean the clogged gutters.

"Your wife needs to sign these court documents," Foster said.

"That will not happen today," Papi said. "Or at least not right now."

"What you do mean? Why would you say that?"

Papi stared at the paperwork. "My wife slipped and fell on the ice this morning. She broke her arm and is this minute awaiting treatment at the hospital. Whatever it is you want, you must have it from me. And please do not take long. I would like to return to the hospital quickly."

Foster frowned. With a forefinger, she pushed back the nose bridge on her glasses. "I'm sorry Mrs. Soria was injured. I guess that explains why you people missed our meeting this morning."

Papi pointed. "Yes, Jenny slipped on the brick walkway right there."

"Jenny?"

"My wife, Vincenza. Jenny for short."

"Oh. Well, it's unfortunate you didn't call to cancel," Foster said.

Papi and Emily exchanged a querulous glance.

"I'm sorry," Papi said. "I thought my daughter had called, but I see by the expression on her face she assumed I made the call myself. Again, Ms. Foster, we apologize. All of us were very upset."

"My mom was in shock," Emily said.

"Her blood pressure dropped very low," Papi said. "The nurse was worried. It will be several hours before the surgery is performed. That is why I brought the children home. But myself, I am needed. I want to get back."

"I understand," Foster said. "But you should have called and rescheduled. That you didn't is a mark against you. To a judge, it seems irresponsible. But right now I'm more concerned with your wife's injury. How bad is it? When will she be home and fully able to take care of the baby?"

Papi sighed in surrender. "She broke her arm. That is all we know. They brought her out of shock with medication, easily, but the surgeon who will later set the bone has not even examined her yet."

"Can I have the keys to the house?" Phillip said.

Papi obliged. "Let us all go inside."

Uncle Phillip led us across the lawn, ice and melting snow snapping and popping beneath our feet. In the kitchen, Phillip shuffled off with his smart phone while the rest of us waited, standing helpless, until Papi motioned for Foster to sit. Then he pulled a red container of Colombian coffee from the cupboard.

"I have time to make a pot of coffee," Papi said. "I know it is unfavorable that we missed the important meeting. But I hope you can see there was no—"

"Mr. Soria, I don't think you understand the seriousness of this situation," Foster said. "Your wife, daughter and grandchild failed to appear for a court-ordered resolution meeting and didn't—"

"My wife was injured."

"-- and never called to reschedule. That's a violation of our agreement."

"She broke her arm!"

Papi had turned up the volume. But Foster was a pro. She smiled and waited a few beats. "Well, just so you understand, the term we use for babies like Noelle is at-risk. She's an at-risk baby because she had no pre-natal care, because her mother abandoned her, and because three of four family members tested positive for illegal substances."

Papi sighed. "None of that is news, is it? That information was part of—"

"What's new is that Mrs. Soria isn't here, and since she's the only family member who tested clean and thus the only responsible adult who has promised to look after Noelle, we have a major problem. And now we don't know if or when Mrs. Soria will be coming back."

The tan skin on Papi's face grew darker. "Of course she will be back. Today. That is a very silly comment."

"But even when she does return, her broken arm could prevent her from administering the proper care and supervision she and I discussed in our meeting at the hospital. The whole reason Noelle came home was because of promises your wife made to me in that meeting. Exceptions were made."

"She will be back," Papi said. "Today. And her arm will heal."

"In the meantime, drug addicts will be taking care of Noelle."

Papi squinted as if bright sun glared in his eyes. "That is a terrible lie, Barbara Foster. And much too insulting to hear spoken at *my* kitchen table."

"It's the truth," Foster said. "Perhaps a bit blunt. I'm sorry. But I want you to see this situation for what—"

Papi cut her off. "I no longer care what you want. I want you out of my house."

Foster gasped. "Excuse me?"

She was a decent actress, looking honestly surprised by Papi's anger.

"I am certain that you heard me. Get out right *now*. And do not come back without armed guards. You are no longer welcome here."

Foster shook her head so violently her glasses almost fell off. She flung a hand up to catch them. "Mr. Soria, that is *exactly* what will happen. I will bring the deputy sheriff. Probably more than one. And if you interfere, you'll be arrested."

Papi marched closer to the redheaded intruder. He reminded me of Mama the day she bulldozed Foster right out of the house. No wonder Mama and Papi had fallen in love and gotten married. They were a pair. Matching rhinos.

"Good luck with that," Papi said. "Now get out."

Foster rose from our table, her head shaking. Her left hand trembled when she lifted her briefcase-slash-purse. "You don't want to talk like that, Mr. Soria. You don't want to say things that suggest you might be violent. Trust me on this."

"I only wished you luck," he said.

Her mouth set into a grim smile. "Well, there's no need for ultimatums or threats. Any possible state guardianship of Noelle wouldn't last long if you and the other family members start testing clean regularly, and if Mrs. Soria returns from the hospital. Perhaps only a few days or a week. But you need to sign these court appearance papers before I leave."

"You're trying to take Noelle away from us?"

My heart stopped. I held my breath.

"No, no. You're agreeing to appear at a hearing. And even if the judge sides with our assessment, we wouldn't *take her away*. That's not what guardianship is about. These papers I'm leaving explain all the details, but basically one of our safe and approved families would keep Noelle for a few days, perhaps a week or more. It depends on your family's drug tests. They'll have—"

Papi growled until the threatening noises became snarling

syllables, and finally, actual words: "Get out of my house."

Foster didn't move. "Which hospital is your wife in?"

Papi's eyes went pure black. Unseeing. "I said get *out*."

Barbara Foster didn't ignore him this time. She stuffed the last paper in her leather satchel and let herself out. From the front steps, Emily and I watched her red curls bounce across the lawn to her gray Ford. Two crows issued a squawking goodbye, and the fresh, pine-scented air tasted cleaner than ever.

Papi brought Mama home from the hospital in time for dinner. A setting sun threw red streaks across the sky as they parked in the driveway. A neighbor's cat squawked in a winter-bare maple tree and Phillip, Emily and I cheered from the porch. The orthopedic surgeon had arrived earlier than scheduled, set Mama's broken arm in forty minutes without titanium rods or general anesthesia, and proclaimed her prognosis excellent. A flesh-colored plastic cast wrapped Mama's right forearm, wrist and part of her hand, but her thumb and the most extreme knuckles of her fingers protruded. She described herself as dizzy but glad to be home.

"Something smells awfully good," Mama said.

Mama had entered the kitchen like a movie star with her entourage. The air was indeed filled with delicious aromas, a byproduct of some tuned up Italian cooking. Emily had prepared a spaghetti dinner using a jar of Mama's frozen homemade tomato sauce, fresh meatballs, fresh garlic and two pounds of imported semolina pasta. After five months in the freezer, Mama's sauce still tasted better than any local restaurant's.

"Are you hungry?" Papi said.

Mama touched his cheek with her good hand. "Not so much, Papi, thanks. But I'd love to watch the rest of you eat."

Phillip slid into a chair. Papi helped Mama, then sat next to her instead of his regular place opposite. Emily collected knives, forks, spoons, napkins and delivered them from kitchen drawer to our table. She also brought and set out three dinner plates, the dinnerware clicking on the wood. I enjoyed a great view from my sink-based bassinette.

"Mama may change her mind," Papi said. "Bring her a plate, too, Emily. Please?"

"There's one there for Mama," Emily said. "I'm the one who's not eating. I'm going out."

"You are joking?" Papi said.

"No. I'm going to a school dance. Demyan's picking me up in a few minutes. We made plans a week ago."

"When will you eat?" Mama said.

"Demyan's bringing sandwiches."

Papi's jaw worked. "You went out last night. Your mother has had her arm broken, has been through surgery and must now exist in a stiff and awkward cast. You surely do not expect Mama to take care of your baby tonight."

"I know. That's why I made dinner. I figured grandfather could help with his granddaughter tonight."

"Because you made me dinner?"

Be nice if my family would use my actual name. You know, Noelle.

"Yeah. And because this is what Mama promised—that the two of you would act like Noelle's parents. That I could live my life as a seventeen-year-old."

Papi glanced at his wife. "That is what you promised?"

"I did?" Mama said.

"You know you did, Mama. You said you'd be her mother."

"I am certain she did not make that promise after she broke her arm," Papi said.

Mama stood and wrapped her arms around her daughter. "It doesn't matter, Emily. You're right. Your father and I will take care of Noelle tonight and every night if we have to. Every night for the rest of our lives. That's what I wanted. What I asked for. What I said I'd be willing to do to keep you from having her adopted."

Emily returned the hug.

Papi grunted. "Mama, I think you have taken too much pain medication."

Mama kissed her daughter's cheek. "You have fun. Don't worry about Noelle or us. But please don't smoke pot, honey? For Noelle's sake. You have to test clean this week again."

"I'll be good," Emily said. "And home early."

"That is what you said last night," Papi said. "And you were not home for breakfast."

Emily slipped on a fur-lined jacket. "Papi, I'll be home before you go to bed."

ELEVEN

Someone delivered Emily home late. Real late. The car woke me up with its rumbling hot rod engine and bass-bumped speakers playing rap music, and seconds later Emily's voice filtered inside the house from the Soria driveway. With my crib in the hall nook, I could peek into Mama and Papi's bedroom, even read their nightstand clock. Noting the time at 3:13 a.m. and that Mama slept alone in the big double bed, I figured Papi waited for his truant daughter in the den. And considering the earlier discussion between father and daughter, I suspected Papi waited in a salty stew.

Except for a tiny cooking light over the kitchen stove, our small wood-framed house was totally dark. Half a minute passed. The old roof creaked now and then under the weight of slowly melting snow. The forced air heating popped on and off. Finally, the side door opened and closed, and Emily's unsteady footfalls padded past the den toward her bedroom.

Papi's chair in the den squeaked.

Emily screamed.

Mama moaned in her bed.

"This is too late to come home on a school night," Papi said. He'd kept his voice low, trying not to wake up the house. Too late, Papi.

"You scared the crapola out of me," Emily said. "What were

85

you doing, hiding there in the dark like some troll?"

"I am a troll? Your father is a monster? Well, princess Emily, let me explain exactly what I was doing. I was waiting for my underage, pot-smoking, child-bearing daughter, wondering how in God's name she will ever graduate from high school without a few hours of sleep or a few ounces of common sense."

"Can you yell at me tomorrow? I need some sleep."

"I am not yelling. I am not even that angry. What I am is tired of your behavior. We have rules here. Seventeen is young to be on your own, but if you cannot follow the rules and conventions of this house, I want you out."

"Rules and conventions? Oh, Papi, you're so silly."

That pushed Papi's button. He had to take a deep breath before he could answer. "I am silly? *I* am silly? Emily, you have been trouble to us your whole life. Neighborhood parents, the police—this community has complained about you since your brother was born. And I have had enough. I will no longer support such an ungrateful, unhappy person. I want you out of this house. And you can take that bastard with you!"

Pain stabbed my chest. I had trouble getting air.

Emily sobbed. "You're so *mean*."

Mama's silhouette filled her bedroom doorway. The long, loose nightgown made her look as bulky as Papi. "What's going on?"

Emily ran past me into her room and slammed the door.

I cried then, too. The word Papi had used and the pain that word brought me did a lot more than cause breathing difficulties. While it's true I am not born of a legal marriage, I'd hoped Papi would love me. But love should never be mean or cruel. Ever. Like a spear, that word had pierced my chest. Was I bleeding to death inside?

Later, Papi and Mama whispered in bed. Actually, Papi just listened.

"I don't think you understand how I feel," Mama said, "so I'm going to make this plain. If you and these kids don't pass the drug tests, I'm taking Noelle and living by myself. I talked to an attorney and I talked on the phone to Barbara Foster's supervisor. I can do it. I can live by myself and get custody of Noelle, and right now, seeing you and the kids fighting and bitching about everything connected to Noelle, after all the love that little baby has brought us, I see this crap and I think why the hell not, Papi. Why the hell don't I take this beautiful, smart, loving child and leave the rest of you shits behind?"

Listening to that, I worked myself up pretty good. Mad first at everything in general, the unfairness of my life and my birth, maybe the unfairness of everyone's life. I experienced a few harsh thoughts about Papi, my mother Emily, even poor Phillip whose whole life had been disrupted through no action of his own. Finally, my temper focused on the true enemy, that person or thing working hardest against me, Demyan and her influence on Emily. How much better things would be for me if Big Pink did what I'd heard Papi say plenty of times—take a long walk on a short pier.

I kept quiet all night though, didn't ask for another bottle of formula until the sun came up. Not that I peacefully slept the night away. Rather I'd spent the dark hours dreaming up ways to lose Demyan Kinsky, alias Big Pink, the tattooed thorn in this baby's side. My strategic plan involved exposure and humiliation. I figured if I showed Demyan to be the mean-spirited bully and bad influence she was, Mama and Papi would find a way to keep her away from Emily. I couldn't do anything to Demyan directly, but I had a chance of influencing the people I lived with. Yesterday I might have said *my family,* but not after Papi said what he said about me. Mama loved me. She was my family. But Papi and Emily, though she'd improved, both seemed to wish I lived somewhere else, and I couldn't tell if Phillip cared one way or the other. He always seemed so busy, either at school, doing his homework, playing basketball games or mowing the neighboring lawns for cash.

My assessment of the family didn't feel harsh, only realistic. Finally, I had to see things clearly, look at my life the way it really was, not through the tuned up glasses of my inherent optimism. I wanted everyone to love me. But that didn't mean they would. I wanted to spend every Christmas at the Soria's dinner party, but no guarantee existed.

Exactly how to win over Emily by exposing Demyan's nature remained a blank spot on my map. Strategic ideas, yes. But a specific plan, no.

The Soria's front door buzzed at nine o'clock the next morning. Emily and Phillip had already left for school, Papi for work, so Mama and I were alone, the two of us struggling to fold a load of laundry with another pile tumbling in the old, barely working dryer. Papi said they couldn't afford a new one for a month or two.

I couldn't actually fold anything, of course, but Mama said I was great moral support, me smiling at her from the bassinette. The work was difficult for her with the right arm in a cast, and against her doctor's orders. But Mama had a good technique, using her stiff arm like a stationary vise or a hanger. A radio played hits from the '90s.

I'd been awake and in good spirits when the doorbell rang, and since Mama didn't like me being out of her sight much, she carried me with her to answer, set my bassinette on the lamp table near the entrance. Opening up the house revealed bright sunshine outside, loudly chirping of birds and two visitors who immediately killed the mood—Barbara Foster and a uniformed, Seaside County Deputy Sheriff, the man's gun and badge on prominent display. Much more than visible, the weapon was a stunning reminder than armed law enforcement had the authority to shoot you dead should you misbehave in a threatening way. Not surprisingly, a glow of satisfaction shone clearly in Foster's eyes.

"Glad you're home, Mrs. Soria," Foster said.

"I bet you are."

"I'm also glad to see you can handle Noelle so easily with that cast."

"Noelle is the easiest baby you've ever met or heard of, Mrs. Foster. A dream."

"Did your husband explain what I told him…about the court appearance? I managed to impart a little information before he threw me out."

The birds stopped chirping.

"Oh my," Mama said. "Papi didn't tell me everything about that visit, did he? You must have really set off his temper."

"I only needed papers signed. As is the case this morning."

"Why don't you two come inside and sit down," Mama said. "We'll have a cup of coffee."

Foster glanced sideways at the deputy. "Honestly, Mrs. Soria, we don't have a lot of time. The deputy especially. So much crime these days."

"Crime is actually down," the deputy said.

Foster smiled at Mama. "Whatever. I meant to say if you'll read these court papers and sign to appear, we'll be on our way."

"My husband mentioned the conversation he had with you, but I don't think he understood completely. What kind of court appearance? I told him he must be mistaken but he claimed you wanted to take custody of Noelle."

"By signing these two papers, you and your daughter are agreeing to appear in our new Family Court. A promise to appear. Child Services has recommended the state take temporary guardianship of Noelle, that's true, but the family court judge has to approve."

Mama backed up a step. She picked up my bassinette. "We have the right to oppose this recommendation, I assume?"

"Of course, you'll have the chance to speak. The family court judge will listen to everything the family has to say."

"What about legal representation. Am I allowed to hire an attorney?"

"Some families do, although you have to understand, we believe we're impartial observers and have a fairer idea of the child's best interests. The judge usually agrees when the family is caught in a cycle of addiction. They normally can't see—"

Mama held up her hand. "That's enough of *that*. I got your cycle of addiction right here, Mrs. Barbara Foster. Give me that pen and paper."

Mama scribbled her name on the promise to appear. "We'll see you in court."

I liked the lawyer's office a lot better than the doctor's. A lot. The soft leather, polished wood and brass fixtures soothed my eyes. The pervasive calm and quiet eased my childish anxiety at new surroundings. Plus, the furniture and carpets smelled nicer. So did the women. Like gentle, perfumed breezes whispering among the desks and potted plants. Plus, nobody at the lawyer's office wanted to poke my tummy or dig inside my orifices.

"Our firm's representation is not inexpensive, Mrs. Soria," the attorney said. "I would need a check for the retainer today if you'd like me to get started."

His name was Miller. He'd been recommended to Mama by a former board member of the hospital where she'd done volunteer work. As an executive search professional who specialized in fancy, first-rate attorneys, this friend of Mama's could always name the top paid lawyers in any specialty.

"Yes, your secretary spelled everything out before she'd make the appointment," Mama said. "Including the retainer. Here's the check. But I don't want to hand this money over— it's my entire personal savings—unless you promise me I'll be able to keep my granddaughter."

From my bassinette resting on the wingback chair next to Mama, I watched the attorney's head shake. A sinking sensation made me feel heavier that one of those giant boulders people install in their front yards. I knew Mama had been mistaken to come here seeking help. You can't fight the state, even with big bucks and a flashy mouthpiece.

Emily enjoyed private eye novels.

"I'm afraid I can't guarantee that, Mrs. Soria. Too much depends on the results of those new drug tests the judge will be staring at. I hope you've stressed the importance of this at home."

"Of course."

"If the tests come out clean, we have a chance," Miller said. "But the child services complaint suggested your husband might be violent as well."

"That's silly," Mama said. "Ernesto hasn't killed anyone in years."

Mr. Miller stared at her for the longest time. I don't think he understood she was kidding.

TWELVE

The family court judge established our hearing would take place in two weeks, and for Mama, Papi, Emily and Phillip, the time passed with relative ease, each routine hour of their humdrum work or school day drawing the family closer to the appointment in the county's new Family Court. But time dragged miserably and interminably for me. Mathematically, three weeks was a gigantic chunk of my lifetime.

Nights were the worst. Lonely hours in the dark crib, my heart struggling with the torture of unrequited love. So many important people had ditched me. My father Billy had run away before my birth and hadn't called. My mother had tried to have me adopted. My grandfather had called me bastard. Even Phillip, my quiet teenage uncle, had never once held me. In short, I did not see myself as a part of that safe and happy family I'd listened to at Christmas Eve dinner—a special place I'd yearned for every single minute of every day since. I wanted that joyous sense of belonging, that happy feeling of celebrating love, and I wanted that bliss with every thump of my heart.

In the nocturnal quiet of Mama and Papi's shadowed hallway, I often wondered during those weeks how many other babies, children and adults worried about the very same thing—belonging. Billions of people in the world, how many millions believed they would never rid themselves of loneliness? They had no family, no lovers, no friends and no prospects. Me, I hadn't given up. I wasn't even close. But millions of people had, I would have bet, especially after months or years of failed effort. Had they convinced themselves, why try at all?

I shook off this infection the same way every night—by remembering Mama loved me, then concentrating on that, recalling ways she'd displayed her feelings. The fire in her eyes being the biggest. That Mama had fought for me to come home and had promised to take care of me, that was evidence. Important evidence. But the love in her eyes was visible proof.

Common sense told me to be grateful for that, and mostly I was. Only late at night, alone in that crib, sometimes I faltered.

Maybe in the dark of night I'd been too harsh on Phillip and Papi, too. Phillip was only a baby himself, really. He didn't go around hugging *any*body. And I didn't think Papi meant to hurt my feelings with what he'd said. First off, he didn't know how hard I listen and how well I understand. Also, being of a different generation, Papi had been teased and was socially embarrassed at work for having an illegitimate grandchild. Yes, he'd used a cruel word he couldn't truly appreciate because of his own legitimacy, but admittedly Papi had smoked more marijuana than he'd let on with Mama. Losing his temper like that could be considered addictive behavior. That he lacked joy over my arrival was not a surprise. Babies were not inexpensive, and his wife had become busier, less concerned with him.

But while I had plenty of worries to keep me up—I was, after all, an at risk child—only one person frightened me. Only one individual actually worked physically against what Barbara Foster called my best interests.

On nights I dreamed of Demyan and her pink, spiked hair, the subconscious images evolved quickly into nightmares.

On her mom's second-hand computer, Demyan Kinsky pulled down the curser, highlighted PRINT and clicked the mouse.

When the old Hewlett-Packard ink box finished rattling, Demyan sealed her bombshell news inside a plain #11 envelope and addressed the front. Block letters. Red ink atop Seaside County's Courthouse street number. The words *Family Court* jumped off the white envelope like a child's bloody cry for help.

Demyan applied a flag-decorated forever stamp and walked her letter down to the apartment's street-side mailboxes. On her way back, she considered the consequences of her mail, particularly that her friend Emily would suffer. But Demyan could see her friend became more attached to that kid each day, and Emily was way too young to be a parent. So was Billy. Also, Billy had his career to think about. Demyan saw these things clearly while her friends were emotionally too young. They needed her help.

When she returned to the apartment she shared with her single mother, Demyan yanked a geometry school book from under the bed. Turning the hardback upside down, she fingered the dangling pages until what she wanted tumbled onto her rumpled sheets. The five-by-seven-inch photograph easily qualified as her favorite picture of Billy, a laughing shot with his shirt off. This bare-chested photo was the only picture she'd ever deleted from her smart phone, the only shot she'd ever had printed, the only one she would never share.

She stared at the likeness of his face while she punched up Billy's house phone and went over her planned speech. Billy's father answered on the fourth ring. "Hi, Mr. Wallace It's Demyan. Billy's girlfriend. Well, one of them anyway...the skinny one with pink hair?"

"Oh, yes," he said. "Pink hair and lots of tattoos."

Demyan laughed. "Guess you saw them all that one morning, huh?"

"Billy said I missed one."

"Hard to believe. But anyway, Mr. Wallace, I called because I was hoping you'd give me Billy's new phone number. I know he's trying to stay away from the people, places and things he knew here, but...well, I have information he'd want to hear."

"You got yourself a new tattoo?"

Demyan stared at a dull gray bird outside the apartment window. She thought it was called a cowbird. No colors at all. "Please, Mr. Wallace, don't be mean. I care about Billy and I'm sure he'd want to know his child is about to be taken by the state. For child abuse. His baby girl is with an awful family."

"What are you talking about?" He hiccupped. "Billy doesn't have a child."

"Yes, he does, Mr. Wallace. Ask the child's mother if you don't believe me. Emily Soria. She goes to our school and I believe you know the family."

"I'll ask Billy next time he calls."

Mr. Wallace sounded tipsy. Maybe drunk. Billy always said his old man loved the martinis and guns, a scary combo. "So you *do* have his number," Demyan said. "Please, can I have it?"

"I don't know the number. He calls on the weekends sometimes. Talks to his sister. I'll tell him what you said next time."

"If he calls her cell phone, she has the number, Mr. Wallace. Please won't you look for me? Ask her. She probably knows the truth about Billy being a father, too."

Mr. Wallace sighed. "Perhaps she did mention something...around Christmas. But let me ask you a question...uh, what did you tell me your name was?"

"Demyan. Demyan Kinsky."

"Right. So tell me this, Demyan, this girl you say is the mother of Billy's baby, Emily Soria. Do you know if she's the daughter of Ernesto Soria, the auto mechanic?

In her new, more flexible cast, Mama gave me a bath before our big court appearance. She wanted everybody to look and smell their best—at the top of their game face, she said—so Mama went room to room checking how everybody planned to dress. She made Emily lose her ponytail and Phillip switch from jeans to dress slacks. I figured all I needed was a fresh set of diapers, but no way. Mama stripped me, sprayed me and lathered me up, hosed my butt off in the kitchen sink. Her hands were gentle and warm, and I enjoyed being the center of her attention. I giggled through most of it, Mama shaking her head at my good nature. Talking to me about the upcoming hearing.

The semi-party atmosphere twisted into a funeral procession after Papi received a phone call. He argued with someone calling from his place of work, but eventually Papi agreed and changed from his Mama-approved court look—a charcoal business suit—into his Chevrolet mechanic's uniform, a navy blue jumpsuit. A Federally mandated recall on certain Chevy trucks had forced cancellation of all vacation days, he told us, and Papi's service manager had threatened to fire him if he didn't show for work. No excuses.

After unloading Papi at his car dealership, the drive to the courthouse stayed quiet and glum. We all understood how bad Papi's non-appearance would look, how much more difficult our objectives became if Papi wouldn't take the time to answer a judge's questions about his alleged violent nature.

Our lawyer had arranged to meet us at the courthouse, and though Mama professed to be confidant Miller would arrange for me to stay with the Soria family, I'd monitored her phone conversations with him the past week, and Miller had seriously played up the family's past drug test failures. So much so, Mama had prodded him about his attitude. And fee. Yes, Miller was talented and expensive, but nothing guaranteed victory, he'd explained, especially if any new drug tests came out positive, or if the Soria family didn't conduct themselves well in front of the judge.

Our Mr. Miller would not be happy about Papi's absence.

Papi not being there bothered me for another reason. Emily, Phillip and Papi had all sworn they would test clean of drugs this week, but who knew? Papi's ditching us at the last minute indicated potential trouble in my book. TROUBLE in all caps, maybe—like Papi knew his test would come out positive and didn't want to face Mama.

As for Emily and Phillip, they'd learned quite a bit about drug addiction in the Seaside County-sponsored classes they'd been forced to attend. I considered their recent behavior encouraging, too, a good sign they'd been staying off the pot and whatever else they'd been experimenting with. In case goodwill helped, I'd been sending out mental vibrations at night to tell them how much I wanted to be a part of their family, and how much I loved each of them.

Something had worked, because Phillip said hello to me in the mornings now, and Emily helped Mama care for me more. She'd even been smiling at me lately, talking to me. I'd worried all along her being nice was only because of Mama's broken arm, but maybe I'd been wrong. I hoped so.

Cars milled about the noisy, crowded courthouse parking lot in search of an empty space. Mama might have taken the last one. Engines rumbled and brakes squeaked. The taste of auto exhaust tickled my throat. Our attorney Miller somehow found us, rolling up on us like ten million dollars in his Ivy League blue suit, white, button-down shirt and maroon-striped tie.

"Where's your husband?" Miller asked.

"Ernesto's boss called this morning and made him come to work," Mama said.

Miller's smile faded. "That's not good."

"Chevy issued a nationwide recall last week. Millions of vehicles. It was on the news. The service manager changed his mind about letting Ernesto off."

"Well, all right," Miller said. "If there's nothing we can do. We'll tell the judge the truth, that your husband is exactly what he is, a hard-working family man that puts his family's security first."

Mama nodded.

Me, I worried about Papi's test results.

After successfully breaching the Seaside County courthouse's old metal detectors and older armed guards, Miller explained the Family Court was located on the upper level of the courthouse's north wing. Use of the one working elevator carried a ten-minute wait, so we scaled the building's cracked marble stairs, Emily lugging me in the bassinette, Mama silently shaking her head with worry. Miller said nothing more about Papi's absence, but since hearing the news, the skin on his forehead had bunched into permanent stress lines.

Watching his and Mama's demeanor, I finally faced the possibility of a court-appointed foster home and living with strangers. Hollowness sucked on my guts. Maybe I'd never see my Soria family again, never spend another Christmas in Mama's happy, loving house. I blinked away tears.

At the top of the stairs, Demyan surprised us, leaping up from a low-slung cushioned chair outside the family courtroom and rushing to Emily's side. Big Pink hugged my mom tightly, claimed she'd come to the courthouse for moral support. There was a twinkle in her eye I wanted to put my finger on—literally—but since I couldn't reach her, I lost control in another way. I let out my first real wail in weeks. Loud.

Shocked faces stared at me.

Mama picked me up. "Oh, Noelle, please, honey. Not now. You have to show the judge how happy you are."

My second shriek disrupted legal minds throughout the courthouse.

Maybe into the next county.

THIRTEEN

I remember contorted eyes and mouths hovering above me, Mama and Emily begging, and then realizing in a flash my vocals only made things worse. I snapped out of my tantrum and abandoned the protest after three or four howls. I can't say the exact number because Demyan's sudden appearance had sautéed my frontal lobes. On top of my stress over what kind of news the judge would deliver, Big Pink being there in all her pierced-tongue glory had over-heated my mental circuitry—to the point of fused connections. Why was she there?

Papi misses court *and* Demyan shows up? What a crushing collection of crapola.

Miller ushered us inside Family Court and sat us on a purple leather bench directly behind his attorney table, a wooden rectangle stacked with case files, loose legal papers and hardbound books. The place smelled like lemon wood polish and gave off a courtroom-*light* mood, probably intentional for the multitude of frightened children who passed through. Despite the familiar and elevated judge's bench, wood paneled walls, and hanging flags, there was no intimidating jury box and no formal bar— that waist-high picket fence—protecting legal eagles from the gallery. In fact, there was no gallery, only the one long row of cushioned benches where we all sat.

Emily placed my bassinette between herself and Big Pink.

Oh, joy. I was helpless and trapped, belted inside that stupid, padded suitcase Emily and Mama called a bassinette, sitting right next to public enemy number one. My hands were free, thank goodness, so if Big Pink tried anything, I could at least protect my eyes. I had no clue what she planned, but I knew Demyan wasn't in that courtroom for any *good* reason.

Judge Carole Terzian, a page-boy blond with piercing eyes and a sharp nose, ran a different kind of hearing than I'd expected—different than anyone would expect if they'd ever watched a courtroom television drama. There was trial-like testimony from Barbara Foster and cross-examination—a little—but Judge Terzian preferred private discussions with the principals in her chambers. First, a state attorney representing Child Services disappeared into the judge's chambers, then our own Mr. Miller. Next, Mama and the social worker Barbara Foster joined the attorneys, and ten minutes after that, the bailiff called Emily into judge's chambers.

Emily got Demyan's attention and signaled toward me. "Watch Noelle, will you?"

Demyan nodded, so Mom left me in my bassinette on the bench next to Big Pink. A warning shot zapped through my nervous system. At least Phillip was close. He sat on Demyan's other side, and as usual, he remained totally quiet. The courtroom contained one other soul, a gray-haired bailiff who guarded judge's chambers with a holstered gun, a badge and a pair of new cowboy boots, maybe Tony Llamas. The county hired retired policemen to save money, Papi told someone on the telephone last night, so there was at least an outside chance the bailiff could protect me.

Demyan leaned close to Phillip. "Stuffy in here, isn't it?"

I couldn't see or hear much of Uncle Phillip. He might have grunted an agreement, or maybe Demyan's stomach gurgled. Hard to say, although Big Pink didn't look like she ever ate enough to produce digestive noises. Underneath those tattoos, Demyan's thin skin stretched across narrow bones.

"The judge won't need you in there," Demyan said. "Why don't you go outside and have a cig?"

Phillip stared straight ahead. "Don't have any."

"I do." Big Pink raided her faux leather purse for a green and white pack of menthols. She dug out two loose cigarettes. "Here. I'd go with you but I have to stay with the baby in case Emily comes back."

Sure seemed like Big Pink angled to get Phillip out of the courtroom. I didn't like contemplating why, though I could not block out her potential crimes. Demyan existed in this world to torment me. I knew that as sure as I knew Emily was my mother. What was Big Pink up to now? I wished Mama Soria would get back.

Phillip accepted Demyan's smokes. "Why not."

The Family Court doors burst open behind us.

Phillip jumped up, hiding the cigarettes. "Papi."

"Billy," Demyan said.

Three men had scuffled in. I recognized Papi's grunt, but I could only guess at the other two. Could Demyan's Billy be *my* Billy—my father, Billy Wallace?

Papi met Phillip where I could see them. He slipped his hand onto Phillip's thicker and taller shoulder. "Where's your mother?"

"With the judge, in chambers. Like everybody is but me."

The bailiff pushed off his paneled wall. "You people need to step outside in the hallway if you're going to have a conversation. There's no talking in the courtroom."

In one polished motion, Demyan snatched my bassinette and soared to her feet. I zoomed higher and swayed back and forth until Demyan presented me to the newly arrived men, a doll in a gift box. "This is your daughter, Billy. And *your* granddaughter, Mr. Wallace."

Mr. Wallace shifted closer. He had white hair and wore nicely fitted clothes. "She's beautiful. What intelligent eyes."

"Yeah, she looks so much like Billy," Demyan said.

Okay, so this was definitely *my* Billy. I hoped he was Billy Wallace the minute Big Pink called his name, and maybe felt a hunch, too. And wasn't it nice to know Billy's white-haired father had such wisdom, intellect and excellent taste?

When Billy and his father both leaned over me, I squealed to make them laugh. Sure the old asset-vs.-liability thing had switched on, but also I could see my father well at that point, and he was even prettier than Emily had claimed, a young man most teenage girls would go soft for. Tall, with a square jaw and shoulder-length blond hair, dark blue eyes and a moody pout to the mouth. Hashtag rockstar.

Hey, I wasn't immune. I wanted Billy Wallace to love me, too.

"Please folks," the bailiff said. "In the hallway?"

I collected a jolting bump against the doorjamb as we all squeezed out. Though she tried, I suppose to impress Billy and his father, Demyan was not as careful handling my bassinette as Mama or even Emily. Always glancing at Billy, Demyan spent too much mental power imagining herself in Billy's arms.

Maybe I didn't understand something. For sure, sex was the topic I knew least about, Emily only having the one experience. Yes, she'd done a lot of reading on the subject, watched the movies, but I couldn't share Emily's personal sensations in the real and imagined moments, only her memories of them. Which like everything else associated with Billy Wallace, Emily had exaggerated into a fairy tale.

I admit I looked forward to love and sex when I grew older. As much as anything else I'd witnessed at Mama and Papi's house, their physical tenderness with each other seemed a most natural and honest expression of love. I understood better than anyone that sex created newborn babies, however, not all of them wanted or loved. Unless they were prepared to raise children, sexual participants should act in a precautionary manner.

Demyan staged my bassinette on a hall bench seat outside

the courtroom and encouraged an adoring Mr. Wallace to show me his car keys. They were shiny and jingled pleasantly, but no way was I taking my attention off Demyan. She'd pulled Billy away and whispered a story in his ear. Minutes passed. Long minutes. Must have been a big story with a beginning, a middle and an ending. A blockbuster finish. Whatever. Big Pink said, her words caused my father serious worry. When Billy turned to stare at me near the end of her murmured dialogue, deep furrows plowed his forehead.

"Hey, Pop," Billy said. "You and I need to talk."

Round and made of white oak, the courtroom's old-fashioned wall clock ticked off the minutes one at a time. The conclusion of each sixty-second period filled the hushed chamber with a loud click, the long hand of the clock snapping forward and ratcheting the tension another bump higher. We'd been waiting hours for Judge Terzian to resolve our fate, although maybe the minutes only *seemed* like hours because I wanted so badly to remain with the Sorias. My gut instincts did not warrant optimism.

Papi and Emily both issued an audible sigh of relief when the bailiff told us to stand. There were additional contented noises including a breathy 'finally' from Demyan as Judge Terzian sat down behind her bench. My bassinette rested between Big Pink and Emily again, but this time the three of us rested across the aisle from Mama and the newly arrived Papi. Mama had been happy to see him, even after he'd explained where he'd been, reasons and clarifications I couldn't hear.

I didn't know what happened to Billy and his father. Mr. Wallace had known Family Court was completely open to the public, but instead of coming inside with us, the two Wallace men had remained in the hallway. Following Demyan's whispered tale to Billy, father and son had engaged in an excited conversation of their own. I worried what Demyan had told him, of course. But I had a preeminent problem in black robes.

"Thank you for your patience," Judge Terzian said. She raised a fist to her mouth and coughed in prelude to speech. Drama queen. "As with many cases this court deals with, the best interests of Noelle Soria are not easily determined. There are at least two sides to every story and both can present compelling evidence and reasons for support."

"Excuse me, your honor," Mama said, "but this is my husband. He—"

Judge Terzian slammed her gavel. "Do not speak again, Mrs. Soria. Listen."

"But your honor—"

"No buts, only contempt of court if you speak again."

Papi wrapped his arms around Mama's shoulders. "Jenny, please."

"As I said, these decisions are difficult, complicated, and sometimes temporarily heart-breaking," the judge said. "But a choice must be made, a decision reached on the child's behalf. We are always reluctant to remove a child from their natural home, especially when I can see the adult acting as the primary guardian is sober, responsible and loving, someone who would keep Noelle's best interests in the forefront of her thoughts and actions."

Judge Terzian paused to take a breath and every soul in that room knew what came next.

"However," the judge said.

FOURTEEN

Judge Terzian paused to breathe. Again. Maybe she was an amateur thespian. "However, in this case, I believe Noelle must be at least temporarily protected from the pervasive and ominous drug abuse that currently plagues the Soria family."

The judge sure enjoyed her adjectives, adverbs and other modifiers, not to mention long pauses, but when she said the words *drug abuse*, my internal commentary abruptly failed due to a startling surprise: Myself and my bassinette were in sudden transit again, whisked from my seat and thrown into rapid motion by none other than Demyan.

What was she doing *this time*?

The judge slammed her gavel. "That child cannot leave the courtroom, young lady."

Demyan and I hightailed it for the courtroom double doors, Big Pink sprinting, me swinging back and forth in her grip like a plastic bag of groceries. I heard gasps behind us, then footsteps. Papi's feet burned the floor chasing us.

"Bailiff," the judge said.

I heard people landing on their feet, shouting—Emily, Mama and Mr. Miller—but Demyan had me out of the courtroom before anyone could stop us. My heart pounded like a jackhammer, sure, but only from surprise and shock. Demyan sported a history of quick, irrational behavior. Looked like Big

Pink was up to more crapola.

Waiting barely outside the double doors was Mr. Wallace and Billy. They seemed prepared for Demyan's excited arrival. Billy reached out for me. Was there some kind of plan going on here?

"Get going, you two," Mr. Wallace said. "Mr. Soria and I will slow them down."

Billy tugged me away from Big Pink. "This way."

My father wore his long hair tucked beneath a Yankees baseball hat. He carried me with two hands, producing a much more pleasant, safer ride, even though Demyan had forgotten to buckle me in after Mr. Wallace had taken me out of the bassinette to hold me and show me his keys. I'd been on the verge of falling out since Big Pink snatched me off the courtroom bench. And although Billy's conveyance ranked much steadier, where was he taking me?

I have to admit, a pleasurable thrill raced through me. In a way, I was delighted to be kidnapped by my father. Scared, too, sure, but Billy's actions only made sense if he loved and wanted me enough to steal me from the law. Armed men and women probably chased us that very second.

"Where are we going?" Demyan said.

That unnerved me. I'd figured Demyan for the mastermind, but then realized my future was five-hundred watts brighter under Billy.

"I don't know yet," Billy said.

Or maybe not.

"But we need to get out of here," Billy said. "Come on, hurry."

Billy knew the courthouse. We descended the public stairway, but only one floor to level two, not all the way to ground level. There were no public courtrooms on the second level, only offices and people-staging areas where potential jurors gathered. The public filled out forms in the county's attached office building, then passed through security to wait at even longer tables for a courtroom assignment. The second floor reminded me of Emily's high school cafeteria, only with no monitors. With a trickle of others, we exited the courthouse for the attached office building, Billy carrying me past the armed guard and metal detectors stationed at the second-floor passage. The guard focused on the people coming inside the secure area, not those of us leaving. On the other side, Billy jogged straight for the polished brass restroom signs. Demyan stayed close.

"The women's head is exactly like the men's," Billy said. "There's a back door for the janitors and a hallway. Find that hall. We'll meet you there."

The men's restroom constituted a new experience. How could these men stand so close together and pee at the same time? I would expect regular if accidental spraying, maybe the occasional fist fight.

EMPLOYEES ONLY had been stenciled on a black-painted door at the rear, but the handle clicked for Billy and he carried me into an empty hall more like a tunnel. Cement walks with drains and whitewashed plaster walls contrasted to the shiny wood and waxed marble of the old building's public corridors. Instead of shaded wall lamps, caged overhead bulbs lighted our way and bits of paper trash lined the floor. The air was stale and offered the faint smell of garbage. Tiny feet scampered in the darkness.

Demyan appeared through a door our left. "Jesus."

"Shush," Billy said. "Come on."

He carried me to another, narrower stairway. Like the service hall, our escape route down to the ground floor was utilitarian, not fancy for the public—painted, scuffed cement stairs instead of white Italian stone, steel pipe handrails instead of polished oak. A strong odor of tobacco smoke led us lower.

At street level, a bedroom-size space off the hall contained two men in gray jumpsuits. Both smoked cigarettes and drank coffee at a battered wooden workbench, a tiny rest area amid a collection of mops, brooms, trash cans and various vacuum cleaners. They watched us pass in silence.

Across the hall, behind a floor-to-ceiling screen barrier, four human dishwashers rinsed stacks of plates, cups and glasses, then stuffed them inside rubber-slotted racks. Another worker loaded the racks inside a stainless steel washer the size of a walk-in closet. These dish-rinsing humans—three guys and one woman—worked in the extreme rear of a massive and wildly busy food kitchen behind the county's employee cafeteria. Huge overhead fans sucked out heat and smells.

"My father worked this cafeteria as a kid," Billy said. "Washing dishes right there. But don't stop. Come on."

Billy led us into what seemed a dead-end. But the black wall slowly became a truck-size garage door that rolled up into the ceiling. "This is the cafeteria's loading dock," Billy said. "It's always locked, but the emergency door over there shouldn't be."

Holding me and the bassinette with both hands, Billy leaned his hip against a four-foot-long horizontal push-bar that opened a steel door marked, NO RETURN KEEP DOOR CLOSED. Sunshine greeted us on the other side, a roofless, cement closet that accessed the loading dock's outside truck ramp. A short hike up the ramp brought us level with the courthouse parking lot.

My heart pounded. I couldn't imagine what they were doing, Billy, Demyan and Billy's father. But somehow I knew Billy loved me. I was more thrilled than scared and I had no idea why.

A gray, two-door Nissan waited for us in the parking lot. The young male driver opened the passenger door and held the seat forward while Billy and I climbed in the back. Billy pointed Demyan into front passenger seat. She wasn't happy. Guess she wanted to join Billy and me.

I know I should have been worried and nervous. Scared. Technically, I was being kidnapped. But what it felt like, I was just having fun with my dad. I trusted Billy Wallace totally. He had my front, side and back—everything.

And what made our playtime even more pleasurable? Big Pink hated it.

* * *

Billy hadn't made room for her, Billy acting salty about the kid, more protective than Demyan had imagined he'd be. But Billy Wallace was Billy Wallace, and at least she was laced up with him, part of his gang. Demyan plopped her butt onto the blue Nissan's front passenger seat and hoped the surprises from Billy were over.

A little luck, she was on her way to Hollywood, even if things weren't going exactly perfect. When she'd asked Billy outside the courtroom where they were going, Billy should have said Los Angeles, his new home, not claim he didn't know their destination. Where else would he take his daughter but where he lived, a move the Soria family would go broke trying to counteract? Los Angeles was bigger than most foreign countries. Maybe Billy didn't want Nick to know. Nick was the driver.

"Where are we headed?" Nick said.

"Emily's house," Billy said. "You know where that is? Over by the hospital?"

"Sure."

Demyan twisted to stare at Billy. What was going on? Her mind thrashed like the Nissan's loose exhaust pipe. "Why the Soria house? What are we going to do over there?"

Billy didn't answer. His thumbs worked hard on an iPhone.

"Are you texting her?" Demyan heard the panic in her own voice.

"I am," Billy said. He didn't bother looking up at her. "I have to tell Emily and her family what happened, that everything's okay."

Demyan choked. How had she fooled herself so badly? "Billy! I thought you were listening to me. Emily...that whole family...they're all addicts."

This time Billy's steady blue eyes rose to examine her. The sexy blond hair slipped back over his shoulders. Crap, he was a hunk. "I'm not taking Emily's baby," he said. "But Pop and Mr. Soria and I all agreed this morning, no way we're going to

109

let the state stash Noelle in some stranger's foster home. Emily's mom will take good care of her. I *know* she will."

Demyan wanted to scream. "But you said you wanted to take Noelle home with you...to Los Angeles. You said the new band was catching on, playing gigs on the Strip."

Billy's head sagged. "Sorry about that. I don't live in Los Angeles. My move out there, the new band...it was a cover story my parents made me tell my friends. Really, I was in drug rehab for six months. A Florida lock-up."

Demyan held her head with both hands. "Holy shit!"

"I know, I know. Sorry."

Demyan could not believe it. "Are you staying at your parents now? Let's go there."

"I live with an uncle upstate. A cop."

"Have Nick drive us *there*. Anywhere but the Soria's."

"Nick will drop you wherever you want after," Billy said, "but first we're taking Noelle home to meet with her mother."

Demyan swiveled to stare through the Nissan's dirty windshield. She'd made some horribly dumb mistakes in her life. Too many to count. But this one topped the freaking list. What a disaster. Her dream of Billy taking her to Los Angeles to help him look after Noelle, maybe singing in his band, was...well, exactly that. A dream. A fantasy. She was dumber than Emily.

Two blocks from the Soria's home, facing yet another week of the early shift at the sandwich shop, Demyan drew a deep, determined breath. Billy still had at least one more bombshell to weather. He could change his mind about Emily and that kid.

And maybe she could throw a little *more* gas on Emily's bonfire, too.

Warm southern air had invaded that morning, chasing the worst of winter, and by the time Nissan Nick dumped us at the empty Soria house, Billy decided we should enjoy the sunlight while we waited for the family. He positioned me on a cushioned wicker loveseat at the far end of the Soria's sunny veranda, a seating area that stretched across the face of the house. Way too big to call a porch. Billy unzipped and loosened my jacket so I wouldn't get too hot, but like Demyan, he didn't notice the bassinette's unfastened containment strap.

Demyan lit two menthol cigarettes and handed one to Billy. "What are you going to say when they get here? Mrs. Soria— Mama, Emily calls her—is going to rip you a new butthole. I can't imagine what her husband's going to do to you."

"I can," Billy said. "He's going to do nothing. Maybe shake my hand."

"What are you talking about?"

"I told you. Emily's father was in on it. He met with me and my father this morning. Told his family he had to work, but the three of us had breakfast and talked about what we'd do if the judge ruled the state would take the baby. Mr. Soria was upset, too."

"That's not the story you spun me first...before I took that baby for you. Why didn't you tell me the family was in on it? Why would you lie to me?"

"You wouldn't have been scared, run so fast, or acted the way you did. That's why Emily's father kept the secret from his wife, too. The family wasn't in on it, just him. Hopefully, he explained quickly after you ran out. I wouldn't want Mrs. Soria mad at me. Jesus. Ripping my butt would be the least of it."

"Nobody's going to be pissed off?"

"The judge and that red haired nerd from child services, sure. Maybe some foster family looking for extra bread in bad times. But not the Soria family. Mr. Soria didn't know *exactly* how his wife would react, but the two grandfathers and I had a plan and Emily's mom should like it. Mr. Soria said she was real worried about losing Noelle, even for a little while. I was, too. I've read bad stories online about those foster homes."

Demyan threw her stubby cigarette on the Soria home's foundation planting of clipped and barren rose bushes. "There has to be more to this story. What's the rest of it, Billy? What didn't you tell me yet?"

"Nothing."

"Come on. Are you going to marry Emily?"

"No. She's seventeen. Maybe in a couple of years. Right now I can help take care of Noelle financially, start savings accounts for her college, that kind of stuff. My dad promised to help."

"But maybe you'll marry her in a couple of years?"

Demyan's sneer was as grotesque and repulsive as anything I'd ever seen, including the horror movies Emily and I watched on television. For utter contempt and total sociopathic contempt for human life, Big Pink's mouth presented an image worse than the wolf man—a curl of the lip that made fangs and fur look kind.

"So what changed?" she said. "A few months ago you wanted nothing to do with Emily. At least that's what you told me while we were...you know."

Billy shrugged.

"While I was..."

His glare made her stop.

Demyan lit another cigarette and examined her nails. "It's the baby, isn't it—that puking, crapping, drooling blob made you fall in love with having a family."

"She's a life, a human with her own future."

Demyan quit staring at her nails to roll her eyes.

"And I created her," Billy said. "Until she's grown and can take care of herself, this little lady is my responsibility."

Billy grinned at me, and I recognized the blaze. I'd seen the same natural brilliance every day in Mama's glances. Those fatherhood chemicals and hormones Emily studied in science class had worked well on Billy, apparently. Filled his blood with devotion. Billy had made promises to his father about me before our meeting, stuff about being drug free and finishing school. But one hour of carrying me around, the poor man was love-struck. He couldn't stop looking at me and grinning.

He didn't notice Demyan texting on her phone.

FIFTEEN

When Papi's 1961 Chevy Impala pranced into the driveway, Billy scooped my bassinette off the wicker loveseat and hurried to meet the Sorias. Mama had big questions written across her face, but Papi must have successfully explained most of what happened on the drive home because Mama wasn't kicking or puffed up like a rhino. She looked worried though, watching Billy approach, and she didn't smile until she held my bassinette.

Mama's cozy greeting warmed me, body and spirit, and in return I unfurled a mighty, gum-filled grin. Warm sunshine radiated between us, her eyes focused on mine. "You scared the crap out of me, Billy Wallace," she said. "But apparently not your daughter. I thought easy-going was Noelle's trademark, but look at this beaming face. You sired one hard-faced gal, here. A tough old soul." She leaned in, touched her round-tip nose against mine. "Look at you. You're smiling like you had a wonderful time."

I did. Fantastic. As I've said, the events were more exciting than scary because I never worried Billy wouldn't protect me. It's one thing to be held and shielded by your mother, or your broken-armed, fearless grandma. But the experience was quite different—more like an adventure—when carried off and safe-guarded by your tall, strong father.

And I'd known immediately Billy Wallace loved me.

Mama lifted her new flexible cast and poked a bare fingertip into Billy's shoulder. "That was some stunt you and your father pulled. The judge almost didn't let your father go."

"They didn't arrest him?"

"No. He's on his way here now," Mama said.

Papi chimed in. "He could be charged later with obstruction of...of something."

"I can't believe they didn't arrest him," Billy said. "I figured he'd spend at least one night in jail."

"You texted Emily just in time," Mama said. "The police had handcuffed your father and were about to issue a statewide alert."

Billy sighed. "I let Emily know as soon as I could."

"Like I said, just in time."

"So my dad's coming here?"

"That's what he said. Listen, the biggest thing on your side— I still have this little bundle of joy."

Mama grinned at me again. I'm not sure she'd ever stopped.

"So what's next?" Billy said. "Did the judge say anything?"

Mama kissed my nose. The bleached whiskers on her lip tickled my forehead. "I texted her as soon as we saw you and Noelle here, as promised. We'll see what happens next."

"You told the judge Noelle was with her father?"

"I told the judge *everything*. I couldn't keep Noelle's location a secret. Your identity either."

"Sure," Billy said.

"All of that information calmed the judge," Papi said. "Not only who you were, and what you texted Emily, but that Mama believed you. I could see the judge was quite impressed with my wife."

"Emily never told us your father was Ernesto's boss," Mama said. "That he owned the Chevy agency."

"I never told her," Billy said. "Demyan knew. She and Emily were always together. I figured...you know. Think my Pop will go to jail?"

"I don't know. There'll be trouble for you, too—more trouble for all of us, I'm sure. I have no intention of bringing Noelle back to that court so child services can take her away. The judge based her decision on false information. I know it."

Billy glanced at Papi. "I'm surprised the cops didn't follow you."

Papi slipped his arm around Mama's waist. "I was thinking that as well. We should get off the front lawn and into the house. The judge said she trusted you to bring Noelle back, but that could have been a ruse or she could change her mind. I am afraid the sheriff or bailiff may come for her any minute. We must decide what to do."

"What about our attorney?" Mama said. "Miller. Shouldn't we ask his advice?"

Papi's head wagged no. "I believe we must leave him out. As an officer of the court, he cannot help if we decide to ignore the judge's orders."

Emily and Billy glanced at each other off and on, maybe not wanting the other one to catch them looking. But when Mama and Papi huddled inside with a newly arrived Mr. Wallace, and Phillip followed, my uncle already on his phone, Billy told Demyan he wanted to talk to Emily. Alone. Big Pink walked away salty. Emily carried my bassinette over to the wicker loveseat and sat beside my father.

"I tried to see you the next day," Emily said. "You know, after your...whatever. But the hospital or your dad or some-body wouldn't let you have visitors. I really tried."

Billy stared at his green kicks. "He didn't believe me—that you saved my life. My dad always thought I was the victim. That my friends were the bad influence." He snuck a peek at her. "They know better now."

Emily wanted to hug and kiss him. I could feel her infatua-tion—the same sense of worship she gave off when making

115

those big red hearts with his initials inside. Her passion burst in the air all around us, filling the afternoon sunshine with imaginary, cartoon love bubbles. I wondered if Billy sensed her effervescence the way I had.

But Emily wasn't done flooding me with thoughts and memories, sending out other images and sensations. Billy's closeness, maybe his voice, had broken some kind of dam inside my mother. After all this time not seeing him, the sight and smells of Billy had tuned up her memory as well as her emotions.

With the first images she sent me, I understood why Billy had been in the hospital.

"How have you been?" Billy said.

In flashes blocked for most of a year, Emily recalled a teaspoon, a cotton ball, a two-inch, plastic bag containing black goo, a length of rubber cord and a syringe with an orange-tipped hypodermic needle. The images gripped her violently.

"Emily?"

The mental pictures came from that night so many months ago when, after making love to Emily in the band room, Billy had used a cigarette lighter to heat the black goo inside the spoon. He'd wrapped his arm with the cord, deliberating cutting off the circulation, and when the black goo liquefied, Billy sucked the molten Mexican tar heroin into the syringe through the cotton ball. He squeezed out an air bubble, stuck the needle into the crook of his arm and released the cord.

On the porch of her parents' house, Billy touched her shoulder. "Emily? You okay?"

The blocked memories blasted Emily's mind, ricocheting like bullets. And there were more. Firing at her, blasting up from her subconscious.

After vein-shooting the Mexican black tar heroin, Billy had smiled at Emily in the strangest way. Drunken and dreamy. But a second later, the blue in the center of his eyes disappeared. Her heart thumped as she stared only at his whites. Like a zombie movie.

From his cross-legged squat, Billy had tipped, then fallen over, forehead slumped near the floor. Emily reached for him.

He'd been unconscious, so she'd shaken his shoulders and slapped his face and yelled in his ears. But Billy wouldn't open his eyes.

She'd checked his pulse. Slow and weak. His face looked a little blue.

Emily had called 9-1-1 on Billy's phone and stayed with him until the police and emergency medical team arrived. The band room had seemed like a cave. She worried they'd never find her.

"Emily! Wake up. Emily! You're like in a trance."

She'd been treated badly by the cops and the emergency medical crew, like Emily was the one who sold Billy the heroin. But she shook off the memories, pushed back the hours spent in the back seat of a police car.

"Sorry," she said.

Emily and I were packing minutes later in her bedroom when the law caught up, me still in shock over what Emily had remembered. I'd always had a hunch the blocked memory involved drugs, but my father Billy shooting up with heroin?

Emily had stuffed clothes and toiletries for both of us in a single suitcase, and with Mama naming herself bus driver and trip coordinator, the three of us planned to escape that night in a rented car. With throw-away phones like spies in a movie. But the screech of police cars—two-dozen shrieking tires, in fact—put a big hold on that flight plan. What would Judge Terzian do when she caught us trying to run from her authority?

We could see the cops out Emily's bedroom window. Three sheriff squad cars filled and blocked our tiny driveway and three municipal black and whites choked the street directly in front of our house. All the flashing red lights and jogging, armed blue soldiers, our neighbors' thoughts must have included multiple homicide or terrorism. How crazy was this scene, that the hub-bub was all about me? A little baby who wanted her mommy.

Mama saluted Barbara Foster and a platoon of deputies on our doorstep. Emily and I stayed out of sight in the kitchen, Emily carrying the bassinette while she tip-toed close enough to hear. She placed the weight of me on Mama's kitchen table, but kept her grip. She still hadn't noticed the retaining strap was unfastened.

"By court order, we are here for Noelle," Foster said. "These sheriff deputies and I sincerely hope there won't be a problem."

"What are you talking about?" Mama said. "The judge's clerk texted me that the hearing had been re-scheduled for tomorrow, an emergency session. You know that test coming back positive on Emily was wrong, and the judge agreed there had been an issue.

A sheriff deputy took a step closer. "We need you to stand aside, ma'am."

Mama didn't budge. "We'll have the baby back in court, and if the judge says so, we'll turn Noelle over to child services then."

"You did a fine sales job on the judge," Foster said, "convincing her you'd have the child back in court, but that's not good enough now."

"What do you mean?"

"The judge changed her mind under new evidence. She received a tip the child's mother is using heroin again—today—and that the family—you in particular—plan to remove Noelle from the state."

"What tip?" Mama said. "A tip from who? You have no right to barge into my house because of a tip, a tip that's a damned lie."

"Sorry, ma'am." The two sheriff deputies crossed the threshold, forcing Mama to the side and then back.

"Hey," Mama said.

Mama's voice squeaked, and that was a starter's gun for

Emily's feet. She and I were in motion before Emily's next heartbeat, my mom hauling me toward the rear of the house. The screeching police cars must have already headlined the news to Billy, Papi and Mr. Wallace, because the three of them met us at the back patio door. Demyan and Phillip watched from backyard lawn chairs. Frozen.

"We have to get Noelle out of here," Emily said. "They're here to take her."

"It is much too late," Papi said. "We cannot run now."

Emily sobbed. The bassinette shook. "We have to."

Papi's head shifted side to side. "The police are here."

We could all see and hear the deputies' invasion. They weren't wearing SWAT team boots, but the footwear qualified as battalion strength. Sounded like a professional football team in metal cleats, spreading throughout the house. We were seconds from being discovered.

"I know what we can do," Mr. Wallace said.

My heart skipped when Billy's father produced a snub-nose revolver from under his jacket. Papi's jaw sank to his chest. His eyes expanded into perfect circles. I guess if you're at all experienced with weapons and the damage they do, their presence can be emotional. For me and Emily, the gun only produced a sense of fantasy. Deadly weapons belonged on television.

"You have a room in this house with no windows?" Mr. Wallace said.

Papi won control of his jaw. Barely. "What? What are you talking about?"

"I said, do you have a room in this house with no windows?"

"No," Papi said. "And I will not let you do anything like what I think you are thinking. I mean, I do not want a weapon in this house. Give me that—"

Papi cut himself off as the first deputies showed up. The little space where we'd gathered, a stepdown between screened patio and backyard, filled with people. A tall and wide-shouldered officer stared at me in my bassinette. More deputies and Barbara

Foster collected behind him, Mama lurking as rear guard to the posse of police. The law behaved calmly, so Wallace must have successfully hidden his gun. At least temporarily. The deputies would have been tugging at their holsters and shouting if they'd seen his weapon.

"Is that the Soria child?" the first deputy said.

All of us remained quiet. But behind the barricade of deputies, Barbara Foster said, "That's her. That's Noelle."

Amid shouts, Mr. Wallace snatched me and the bassinette from Emily and scurried into the hall bathroom. I teetered and tottered, darn near falling out, but I managed to hold onto the bassinette's rails as he whisked me away. If someone didn't notice my unfastened belt soon, I feared personal injury. No fun being the football everyone's chasing and throwing toward the end zone.

Papi thrust a hand out to grab me but he was too late. So was the deputy who lunged after us. For his belated effort, the county cop had the bathroom door slammed in his square-jawed face. I was inside the bathroom with Mr. Wallace. A herd of men tromped closer, and the bathroom door shook. But Mr. Wallace had already locked it. A fist pounded. Wood rattled. "You are endangering that child, sir. Open this door."

"You're going to scare her shouting and pounding," Mr. Wallace said.

His words must have been muffled by the door, but I hoped the deputies heard his voice crack. Mr. Wallace was frightened and I believed that information could help them. I rooted for the deputies because I had no clue what Wallace planned or might do with that pistol. I didn't want anyone to get shot.

The door quit rattling. Wallace used the respite to slide down the window shade. Next he shut the toilet lid, then set my bassinette on top. His fingers trembled holding the gun, a short-barreled revolver like police detectives carried in a couple of the old movies Emily had watched. I tried to snuggle my butt deeply into the bassinette in case I slipped off the toilet or bullets started flying. I'd understood why Wallace's hands shook when a single fact sunk in: His weapon was not pretend. This ugly little scene was not part of a movie.

Over the next twenty minutes, various people tried to reason, cajole or threaten Mr. Wallace through the locked bathroom door. Mama begged him to put my safety in front of his macho protection act. My dad Billy pointed out the number of cops on hand and the virtual certainty Wallace would be shot or arrested. Emily cried for her baby back. And finally, a late arrival, one of Judge Terzian's court clerks, verbally added up the potential jail time Wallace would earn by the end of his "silly and ineffectual meltdown."

But Mr. Wallace stayed barricaded.

Mama dynamited the logjam when, through the clerk, she contacted Judge Terzian. By explaining what had happened, what the family wanted and using the sheriffs and the clerk to back up her facts about present circumstances, Mama convinced the judge to participate in a FaceTime chat. With Noelle being held hostage at gunpoint, Judge Terzian didn't have much of a choice, Mama said. What was she going to do, say no?

"Did you hear the judge, Mr. Wallace?" the clerk said. "All you have to do is turn over the weapon—slide the gun carefully out the door. When we have the weapon in a safe place, you bring Noelle out of the bathroom and the FaceTime meeting will start."

"I heard, but I don't believe it," Mr. Wallace said.

Since there easily could have been conversations the family hadn't heard, say a private talk between the judge and the clerk, Mr. Wallace was not the only one who worried the judge's acquiescence was fraud. I figured as soon as Wallace surrendered he'd be arrested and I'd be hauled off to child services.

But over the next fifteen minutes, Mama and the judge wore down Wallace's misgivings. Judge Terzian patiently convinced him she wasn't busy, the time of day didn't matter, that she desperately wanted to end any threat to the child. That's why she'd told her clerk to show up. If a FaceTime chat would get Wallace to turn over the weapon, the judge promised to hear the family's pleas to keep Noelle out of state custody. And hear those requests right then and there.

I wondered if this was a new police technique, embracing the latest in communication technology to snag the crooks. Oh, Mr. Wallace wasn't a crook—a bad guy. I knew that. He was my grandfather and the poor man only did this to keep me from whatever inadequate apparatus the state had developed to handle *at risk* babies. But the longer we spent in the bathroom together, the more the gun scared me. Emily had seen plenty of news stories. People with guns got shot.

As directed by the clerk, Mr. Wallace first cracked open the bathroom door. We all heard the lock click, and I half expected one of the sheriff deputies to kick in the door and wrestle Mr. Wallace into handcuffs. But maybe Emily and I had watched too much television because that's not what happened. Nothing happened.

Mr. Wallace next pushed forward his revolver, offering the weapon grip first, the cylinder's edge scratching the hall's wooden floor. The gun immediately disappeared from our view.

"All right, Mr. Wallace," the clerk said. "Now bring out Noelle."

Mr. Wallace's fingers trembled on the bassinette. He smiled at me, though. "Here we go, darling. I hope that smooth-talking judge keeps her word."

He tugged on the door. The sheriff's supervisor waited for us in the hall, and gently removed the bassinette from Mr. Wallace's grip. I held my breath, as did everyone else there named Soria or Wallace. Maybe Demyan, too, as she and Phillip watched through a screen door. We all waited for the explosion of violence we expected—that Mr. Wallace would be handcuffed and dragged outside to a squad car.

But he wasn't.

And when Mr. Wallace sat in the kitchen chair Mama offered him, like a witness stand before the computer image of Judge Terzian, I think we all expected the judge to listen maybe two minutes before cutting him off.

But she didn't.

SIXTEEN

Points of irony stuck me that evening, the worst being Mama making coffee for the police in her antique, twenty-six-cup electric percolator she normally plugged in only once a year—at the world's greatest Christmas Eve dinner party. The rich aroma from that old percolator did more than *remind* me of the night I was born, listening to the party as I slowly left my mother, entranced by the Soria family and their friends relishing a joyous holiday. The remembered scent doused my heart with love for the Sorias again. How mocking was it the family court judge might send me to foster care with that night's memory of exhilaration so prominent in my thoughts.

A glue-backed, white cardboard snowflake remained attached to Mama's chrome coffeemaker, a remnant of Emily's childhood enthusiasm for Christmas. I doubted the smell of percolator coffee had the effect on Emily as the aroma did on me, not only because her memories of my childbirth were primarily pain and suffering, but because my mother appeared agitated and concerned. And darn if the object of her worry wasn't little old me. After Mr. Wallace brought me out of the bathroom, my mother had wiped my forehead with a cool, wet paper towel, talking to me the whole time, asking if I was okay and if I needed anything. Like I could talk back. She'd checked my diapers, kissed me multiple times and given me a warm bottle. Emily was acting like a mom. She'd done everything I could have asked but reattach that stupid bassinette's containment belt.

After Wallace surrendered, Judge Terzian had gone off-camera a few minutes. On her return, her hair looked neater and a hint of lipstick shaded her mouth. Her cheeks might have been a touch rosier as well. Maybe she had a thing for our attorney, Mr. Miller, who she'd allowed into the chat through his iPhone. When she was ready, the judge coughed to get everyone's attention. "All right, Mr. Wallace, we made a deal. Let's hear what you wanted to tell the court."

Billy's father didn't hesitate. "First, Your Honor, I apologize for keeping you and these sheriff deputies from their families and more important duties tonight."

"I assure you, Mr. Wallace, your actions were—and are—extremely important to this court."

"I'm sorry, Your Honor...I let my emotions get the best of me."

"Screaming profanities is emotional," the judge said. "Threatening people with a gun is more than emotional, Mr. Wallace. It's criminal."

"Have you ever have your first and only grandchild approached by armed men who want to take her away?" Mr. Wallace said.

The judge hesitated. "No, but I've been a family court judge for more than a decade, and I assure you I am well versed in the emotional nature of *everything* this court does concerning children."

"Maybe. But I wasn't even sure I *had* a granddaughter until last night," Wallace said. "Today was the first day I'd ever seen her."

"Is that so? Well then I do understand how you could have become overly emotional. I will recognize that as a factor. But we need to move this conversation forward, Mr. Wallace, and address the issues before us. Why shouldn't the state take temporary custodianship of Noelle? The family has repeatedly tested positive for drugs."

"Wait, that's not right," Wallace said. "Is it?" He glanced at Mama.

"No, that's not right, Your Honor," Mama said. "Only Emily—our daughter—tested positive during the last month. And our attorney said the test was inconclusive—too mild a response for real opioids."

On our computer screen, we all saw the judge glance at documents before her. "My information is that everyone in the Soria family has tested positive for drugs—everyone but Mrs. Soria."

"That was two months ago, Your Honor," our attorney Miller said. "And the reason for child service's initial involvement. In all but one test, the first test, the only drug discovered was marijuana."

"The baby changed everybody," Mama said.

"Well, not everyone," the judge said. "As you've admitted, the mother Emily Soria tested positive again for opioids a few days ago."

"That result was questionable, Your Honor," our attorney said.

"The results were reanalyzed and again conclusive," the judge said. "There were opioids in the mother's blood. The amount doesn't matter."

"The amount registered was so faint, experts claim over-the-counter diarrhea medications or even poppy seeds could have caused the positive response," Miller said.

On screen, Judge Terzian stared straight ahead, her nose moving slightly side to side. "I agreed to hear out Mr. Wallace this evening for the sake of Noelle and to ensure there would be no violence, but I will not reargue the evidence. Mr. Wallace, do you have anything else to add before I summarize and make a decision?"

"I've wanted a grandchild all my adult life, Your Honor, ever since Billy was born. But my wife died and I've never remarried because I loved her much, so Billy is my only shot at grandchildren. Until I found out about Noelle, I didn't think it would ever happen because Billy's been so wild, and I was worried—"

"Not a good topic," our attorney said.

"Your point?" the judge said.

"...I was worried there wouldn't be any grandchildren. Why can't I look after Noelle until child services determines the Sorias are ready for her again?"

"You could apply," the judge said. "But it would take months to get an approval, and honestly, I'm afraid your actions tonight would seriously dampen your chances."

From my bassinette on the kitchen sink, I noticed Demyan had shifted inside the house and squeezed in closer to the action. She maneuvered to see the judge's face. Big Pink carried a tan fake leather purse hooked on her wrist, acting proper and calm, but I was certain Demyan gloated over my upcoming departure. She wanted to witness the judge's ruling from the most advantageous position she could acquire.

"She's my granddaughter," Wallace said. "Doesn't that mean anything?"

"It means a great deal," the judge said, "but there is still a legal process."

"But judge. Please—"

The judge cut him off by raising her hand. "I'm afraid that's all the time I have, Mr. Wallace, Mr. and Mrs. Soria. And I'm sorry, but I must rule Noelle be removed temporarily from the Soria household, and that she should remain in foster care until the entire Soria household can maintain a drug-free environment for ninety days."

Trying to get a better view at the judge, Demyan squeezed closer to my bassinette. I had a hunch, a good one, and since my bassinette strap was still undone, and since I had nothing to lose except an undetermined sentence inside a state-run baby tank—that infamous babysitting system into which dozens of kids, maybe hundreds, had disappeared forever—I kicked with my right foot and rolled hard to the left, flipping the bassinette onto its side, and at the same time, screaming the biggest, loudest wail I'd ever dispensed. Bigger than the one in the courtroom.

There was method to my madness. I had my gaze on Demyan's purse, and all I needed to snag my foot through the strap was for Demyan to pause as she walked close. My scream did it, freezing Demyan and everyone else in the room.

Mama and Emily gasped. Papi leaped toward me. A big deputy grunted. Billy stood closer and athletically grabbed for me as I rolled off the kitchen counter. But most importantly, my ankle had snagged the strap of Demyan's tan purse perfectly, and by kicking my foot again as I rolled off, I tossed that sucker in the air. Upside-down and spinning in slow-motion, Demyan's fake leather handbag disgorged its contents in a rush.

Billy caught and held me as Big Pink's treasures splattered onto the kitchen floor. We all saw a thin red wallet, a cellphone, lip gloss, a crumpled pack of Kool cigarettes, keys, gum wrappers, a wad of clothing store receipts, a hair brush, a half-empty pack of matches, a plastic cigarette lighter, a packaged condom, three rolled joints and several clear plastic pill bottles. One bottle contained hundreds of black dots.

My hunch had been right.

But did anybody else see them? Isn't anybody going to do something?

The sheriff captain reached for one of the joints, held the white, hand-rolled cigarette to his nose and sniffed. "This is marijuana."

Okay, nice job, officer. But there's more. So much more. Don't you see them?

"Are those condoms?" Mama said. Her upper lip curled.

Oh come on you people! Look at the bottles.

Papi picked up a clear container of black dots, popped the cap and tasted one. "Judge, these are poppy seeds."

Mr. Wallace put everything together quickly. He blocked

Demyan's attempt to beat him, then snatched Demyan's phone off the floor. With her protesting, he clicked a few buttons. "This phone shows Demyan was the anonymous source, your Honor. She called the bailiff in your court about an hour ago and texted you this address." He offered the phone to a deputy.

"Clearly, Demyan has a grudge against Emily and the baby," Miller said. "And because she's a close friend of Emily, she easily could have dumped these poppy seeds in Emily's food sometime before the drug test."

"She's been feeding me bagel sandwiches for weeks," Emily said. "Every single one had those little black seeds on top."

Demyan stared at me in Billy's arms. Her hands clenched.

Emily moved beside Billy to look at me. "Are you okay, Noelle?"

I grinned.

Mama raised a hand to speak. "Judge Terzian, aren't there fancier drug tests that could tell the difference between poppy seeds and real heroin use? If the court or child services can't afford them, I'd be extremely happy to pay."

"The sheriffs have a DEA-approved urine test in the supervisor's car," Barbara Foster said. "Or if we clip some of Miss Soria's hair, we could have totally accurate lab results within forty-eight hours."

SEVENTEEN

In Mama's annual forest of lighted Christmas trees, amid her bright-colored army of nutcrackers, angels, reindeer and Santa Clause dolls, thirty of us laughed and teased one another at the Soria's festive dinner table. The joyous sounds warmed and cheered me on the anniversary of my birth exactly like last year's Christmas Eve's celebration, or perhaps even better because Billy and Mr. Wallace were here. Benevolence and love invaded my spirit as before, like musical sunshine, or the dancing rhythm of drums. Emily's family was my family, too, and last year's heartbreak had been stitched and healed. The Sorias wanted me. So did the Wallaces. That I was certain of that made me as happy as a one-year-old child could ever be.

"Blow out your candle, Noelle," my mother said. "But make a wish first."

My name decorated the cake plus the words *Happy Birthday* and a glistening winged angel in mid-flight. The image was no accident. Flinging myself off the counter to toss the contents of Demyan's enlightening purse had been a much talked-about feat all summer and fall. Mama and Papi both said a family legend had been written, a story to last generations. At one point earlier that night, Papi had lifted his glass. "To Noelle, the greatest kicker since Bruce Lee."

"Maybe George Blanda," Abuelita said.

"And the greatest detective since Sherlock Holmes," Mama said. "I swear our little girl knew exactly what was inside Demyan's purse."

My mom—I never thought of her as Emily anymore—didn't know I understood about the wish and candle thing. She'd been kidding about the huffing-puffing part. But I'd been familiar with the simple and widespread birthday tradition because of Emily's birthdays, her memories of them, and secretly I'd looked forward all year to blowing out that candle myself—that is, being the one to make a wish.

But I'm glad I didn't get the chance too soon. I might have wished for a new stuffed toy, sweet-smelling shampoo, or even a ride with Mom to the kiddie park. Knowing everything I knew then, I wanted something else.

I breathed deeply, closed my eyes and I made the biggest, most important wish anyone on earth could ever make. Immortality? The end of war, famine and disease? Nope, even bigger. What I wanted would make all of those things happen anyway. What I wanted would make the world into the place we should have created from the beginning. My wish: That someday every girl and boy born would know love like this Soria family and their friends had given me. What a victory for humanity, a beginning for *everything* this world needed, every good change mankind sought.

So I made my wish. That wish. And I blew on that candle with everything I had.

JACK GETZE is the author of the award-winning, darkly comic Austin Carr Mystery Series, plus a stand-alone thriller, all from Down & Out Books. A retired former newsman, public relations consultant, and telephone-based, municipal bond salesman, Getze understands communications and works hard to make reading easy. The most recent of his Austin Carr novels, *Big Shoes*, won Deadly Ink's Best Mystery Novel of 2015.

On the following pages are a few
more great titles from the
Down & Out Books publishing family.

For a complete list of books and to
sign up for our newsletter,
go to DownAndOutBooks.com.

Noiryorican
Short Fiction
Richie Narvaez

Down & Out Books
November 2020
978-1-64396-120-0

A reluctant assassin is born. A con man tries to sell the Grand Central clock. A superhero is dying to lose her powers.

In thirteen fast-moving stories, the author of *Hipster Death Rattle* explores the tragic world of noir fiction with a wide range of Latinx characters.

These stories define noir as tales of people who fall not from great heights but from the stoop and the sidewalk.

My Funny Valentine
The Rat Pack Series
Nigel Bird

Down & Out Books
November 2020
978-1-64396-131-6

Double Dutch loves playing Cupid and for one lucky lady his arrow will be painfully sharp. Only the police can prevent him from hitting his target before Valentine's Day comes to a close.

It's almost twenty years since the last Double Dutch killing and he's back with a vengeance. The discovery of his latest victim resurrects ghosts the police hoped they'd laid to rest forever. With Valentine's Day almost upon them, detectives know they have limited time to avoid another slaying.

Follow DI Wilson and his team as they try to locate the killer before he strikes again.

All Due Respect 2020
Chris Rhatigan & David Nemeth, editors

All Due Respect, an imprint of
Down & Out Books
November 2020
978-1-64396-165-1

Twelve short stories from the top writers in crime fiction today.

Featuring the work of Stephen D. Rogers, Tom Leins, Michael Pool, Andrew Davie, Sharon Diane King, Preston Lang, Jay Butkowski, Steven Berry, Craig Francis Coates, Bobby Mathews, Michael Penncavage, and BV Lawson.

Deemer's Inlet
Stephen Burdick

Shotgun Honey, an imprint of
Down & Out Books
August 2020
978-1-64396-104-0

Far from the tourist meccas of Ft. Lauderdale and Miami Beach, a chief of police position in the quiet, picturesque town of Deemer's Inlet on the Gulf coast of Florida seemed ideal for Eldon Quick—until the first murder.

The crime and a subsequent killing force Quick to call upon his years of experience as a former homicide detective in Miami. Soon after, two more people are murdered and Quick believes a serial killer is on the loose. As Quick works to uncover the identity and motive of the killer, he must contend with an understaffed police force, small town politics, and curious residents.